MW00885075

MIDDLE SCHOOL MADNESS

BOOK ONE

A Strange First Week

By R.D. Trimble

MIDDLE SCHOOL MADNESS

Copyright © 2018 by Russell Dennis Trimble

All rights reserved.

No part of this publication may be reproduced, distributed, or transmitted in any form or by any means, including photocopying, recording, or other electronic or mechanical methods, without the prior written permission of the publisher, except in the case of brief quotations embodied in critical reviews and certain other noncommercial uses permitted by copyright law.

PRAISE FOR MIDDLE SCHOOL MADNESS

"This book rocks! R. D. Trimble is awesome for caring so much about kids. He is a great writer!"

~ **Bryson, Age 11**

"I really enjoyed this story; it is the beast!"

~ **Devon, Age 12**

"I loved the story!" ~ **Lisa, Grown-up**

"I loved the story, and reading it to my son made my heart smile."

~ **Terra James, Author of** *The Immortal* **series.**

"One of the best books I have read in a while. I was left hungry for more. Great Job!"

~ **Tomás Trinidad, Author of** *Tricka and Magika's Halloween.*

Fun Fact: 99% of the gas your body produces does not smell. Just saying…wow, that one percent must be awful!

PRAISE FOR MIDDLE SCHOOL MADNESS

"This is not your typical Middle School book. I just can't get over how hilarious it is!"

~ Anamaria Robles Ramirez, High School Student

"I liked that it told you about how you go through life and helped you understand how you can get through things like people making fun of you. I like the part where he said pooping was his opinion of bullying.

~ C. W., Age 10

"I liked the book because it shows how to deal with bullies, and it's hilarious, not sad."

~ Dakota, age 11

"That was awesome! I wish I had all the video games he talks about. That school sounds cool, did he go there?

~ Tyler, age 12

"The book is funny and a pretty good story. The father was mean to his son by pranking him. The Foul Wind Blows Chapter 11 was just gross because he farted stinky like 5 times! I like the fun facts and googled some of them to check out more. I would tell my friends to read this.

~ Dionn, Age 11

"If you have a boy in your life over the age of 8, do them a favor and buy them a copy of Middle School Madness by R. D. Trimble. It is full of everything a growing boy

---

Fun Fact: It rains on the planet Venus, but it is made of sulfuric acid!

4

needs. Humor, fun, fart jokes, wrestling, cosplay, swords, outsmarting the bad guys, dad jokes, and oh yeah, did I mention the fart jokes. Being a girl, I was convinced all boys had cooties in middle school. Now I know why. The author manages to get inside the head of the average male middle-schooler and lay it all out for us in a fun and funny way. "

~ **J. D. Lakey – Author of** *The Black Bead Chronicles*

"This book is so amazing! Rusty cares so much for kids!"

~ **Devin – Age 14**

Fun Fact: One theory about the dinosaurs going extinct; climate change due to methane from dinosaur flatulence, mainly from herbivores. I wonder, does that mean dinosaur vegans are to blame?

A VERY SPECIAL THANKS!

It is with a heart full of excitement and gratitude that I give my thanks to the following people (last names omitted for privacy's sake):

- Katy and her children Ava and Evan who lent their names to this book.
- Tom and Sandra along with their children Liam and Marcus who lent their names to this book.
- Terrin and her son Bryson who lent his name to this book.
- Suelean who allowed herself to be cast as Sue (aka "Lady Pain")
- My wife Nickcole and my sons Andrew and Tyler
- My dad Steven (1938-1987) – Miss you!
- To Dr. Fred Ream on whom I based Dr. Raines.

A VERY SPECIAL THANKS!

- Kyndra Mckrola for her proofreading help!
- Gary for letting me use him in this novel.
- Ken Tucker and Sarah Loredo who shared their likenesses and song *Mr. Moon*.
- Lisa A. Boyd for proofreading the first draft.
- Tomás Trinidad (author of "***Tricka and Magika's Halloween*** and "***Hello, My Name is Pepe!***" for proofreading the final draft (you saved me from several huge errors!)

Finally, a message: To any of you who have endured a bully (or bullies) in your life. Hang in there. I know it is rough, but bullies ALWAYS lose in the end, as long as you persevere!

7

FOREWORD

My days in Middle School were not good ones. I dealt with bullies and teasing, mainly because I was different; a symptom of my Autism, which was not diagnosed at the time. I do not ever remember starting trouble with other students, but because I was skinny, shy, and awkward, I was an easy target.

That said, I feel it is important to point something out about this book. Hugo Finley, the main character never truly resorts to violence, and that I feel is very important. However, some of his actions, mainly acts of practical jokes against those who bullied him, are of questionable moral value.

BULLS ARE COOL, BULLIES ARE NOT!

By that, I mean that by no means do I encourage or endorse such actions as Hugo takes here, however funny you might find them (and yes, I think they ARE quite funny). Bullying is a big problem, but ending it I believe starts

---

A Plea to my readers: Bullying takes many forms. Words really can hurt people. Please treat others as you would wish to be treated.

FOREWORD

not with taking matters into your own hands, but rather with speaking to your family, friends, and teachers; let them help you.

With that being said, I hope that you will enjoy this story. If you do, I hope that you will send me a message at rustytrimble@yahoo.com; one can never have too many friends. In the meantime, I say...

Journey on,

R. D. Trimble

E:mail: Rustytrimble@yahoo.com

Twitter: @rustyauthor

Facebook: Rusty Trimble

They are all running to buy "Andrew and the Pirate Cove"! ☺

Fun Fact: The "I" in my signature above has a pirate's cutlass instead of a dot. My first novel was a pirate book called "Andrew and the Pirate Cove". It is available online, check it out sometime.

MIDDLE SCHOOL MADNESS

PROLOGUE

I read earlier in the week about Greek mythology and the peril of staring into the eyes of Medusa, a snake-haired lady who could turn their hapless victims into stone. Well, I can say that is far more fun than gazing into the steely visage of my Tom Harkin Middle School's Principal, Jeff Nottingham.

His green eyes seem to burn into mine through his octagonal spectacles and for a moment, I swore smoke was puffing out from his oversized nostrils. There is one thing that is for certain; he is not happy with me.

Fun Fact: These Fun Facts will be on every page. Some are educational, some tell you about me, some are fun, and others about authors I recommend or good books to read.

A STRANGE FIRST WEEK – by R. D. Trimble

For the record, I am a good kid and I did not set out this morning to get into trouble. This was far from the vision I had for the end of my first week of 6th grade. I do all my homework, raise my hand often in class, and am genuinely nice to everyone. I do not seek to cause problems for anyone and am not a malcontent; which is how I overheard Nottingham describe me as I paced outside his office.

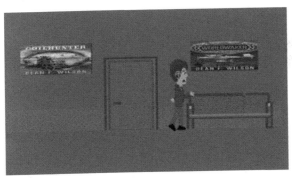

So, you may be wondering how did I end up in this mess? Well my dad always liked to say "Hugo," (that's me, Hugo Finley) "sometimes bad things happen to good people, sometimes good people do bad things, and both happen at once. Hey, sometimes trouble just seems to come knocking on their door like an uninvited guest, kind of like your Uncle Clay and Aunt Kathy."

(Un)Fun Fact: Uncle Clay and Aunt Kathy are based on a pair of former bosses I used to work for.

MIDDLE SCHOOL MADNESS

Uncle Clay and Aunt Kathy are a pair of freeloading, rude, and overall despicable people who I am sad to say are relatives. Fortunately, we moved away and will no longer see them.

Anyways, to return to the present, this is a Friday in the first week of September and I find myself finishing my first week of middle school by being on the receiving end of what I suppose must be Principal Nottingham's own version of Medusa's stare.

I had spent a portion of this week acting the role of a superhero, and had I any power I wished, it would've been to fly on out of this office.

I am mulling again the dreadful gaze of Principal Nottingham. While my body has not turned to

---

Fun Fact: *Medusa* is a creature from Greek mythology; possessing the torso of a serpent and a head with snakes for hair. Looking at her could turn that person to stone!

stone, I think inside my blood has been frozen cold and at the moment, turning into a statue does not seem to be the worst prospect. I dreamed of an epic battle like the one Perseus had, while I awaited my fate.

My dad is on his way down to the school and sadly this is not the first time this week he has had to come down here to see me, it is his third. Yes, I said that; three times! The first week of school; yes, a new school, and I have been sent to the principal every day this week; and Monday alone I was sent several times! Like my dad said, trouble happens. Well...he used a different word

Another Medusa Fact: Medusa's story is tragic as she was changed into her hideous form as punishment for falling in love with Poseidon; the Greek deity of the sea.

than trouble, but I am not allowed to use that word.

Five-plus times in one week is hardly a good start for a new student. However, I can go one better than that by sharing that dad has had to get involved on my behalf even more than that.

In a nutshell, my dad has had to rescue me three times at the Principal's behest, once on account of the police, and once time due to security, though he at least did not have to drive to pick me up, just be escorted from his seat to where I had been taken. At least one of those five I knew had a happy ending of sorts. I am of the idea that this particular visit from my dad will not end exceptionally well for me.

This whole time, Principal Nottingham has been staring at me, "shooting daggers" as my

---

Fun Fact: The snakes that make up Medusa's hair are also poisonous, most stories I have read imply they are asps.

mom would say and not saying a word. I am beginning to wonder if those glasses allow him to look into my soul and to paraphrase a certain famous, golden-skinned robot, I asked myself "How did I get into this mess, I really don't know how."

Well actually I do, but before I can further ponder it, Principal Nottingham has decided he's had enough of the stare down and begins to speak to me.

"So Mr. Finley, I'm really interested in how you think you can talk your way out of THIS mess!"
That makes two of us, but while he is waiting,

Fun Fact: I first heard of *Medusa* when I was ten years old and saw the movie *Clash of the Titans*. I have never seen the 2010 remake of the movie.

the last week of my life begins to flash before my eyes.

Fun Fact: The film *Clash of the Titans* (the 1981 version) took a lot of liberties with the original myth of Perseus.

PART I

A TRULY EPIC WEEKEND!

Shameless Book Plug: *Tricka and Magika's Halloween* and *Hello, My Name is Pepe* by Tomás Trinidad.

CHAPTER ONE

A STRANGE ODYSSEY

My dad always told me that when I need to discuss a problem, well...to start right at the beginning. That beginning I guess is when we packed up my dad's car and my mom's minivan to move to our new home. I had been living in Mesa, Arizona and had endured the worst that the summer had to offer.

Now if you have never lived in Arizona in the summer, let me explain something about it. Yes, it gets hot, VERY hot. However, that is hardly the worst of it. It can be well over one hundred degrees and still rain. Most kids look forward

---

Fun Fact: Strange Odyssey is a reference to the classic computer game of the same name (1981) by Scott Adams and the Honda Odyssey minivan my wife owns.

to the summer, I looked forward to the winter where it rained less and was actually cool outside most of the time.

Anyways my mom is an Accountant and my dad is a software programmer who designed video games. Perhaps you've heard of *Blondes vs Zombies?* It was a smash hit and it was the reason we were moving. He had done this as a solo project, a hobby really and now had a new job from *Mainstream Media Gaming* and so we loaded up our two vehicles and said goodbye to our rental house towards what I heard mom silently describe as an uncertain future.

I think I was the most scared about the trip. I mean I was going to be the new kid at school, a middle school at that, heading into the sixth grade; AND in a new city. I had seen the new kids get razzed a bit and since I was from Arizona, I was sure it'd be double the pleasure. Still, we had a splendid future ahead of us dad said, so off we went.

Fun Fact: Blondes vs Zombies is a spoofing homage to the videogame *Plants vs Zombies.*

CHAPTER ONE

We hired a moving van to carry most of our stuff, so the trip to our new home in San Diego, California would take maybe six or seven hours dad said. We could not dawdle, school started Monday and it was Friday, my last true day of summer vacation; spent in a car as dad's small compact was the only vehicle that had any room for me; mom's car was loaded up with stuff.

It is here where I should've had my first premonition of trouble. I think it is important to know that my dad fancied himself a "Consummate prankster". He was not above waiting for me to watch a scary movie and sneak into the living room with a flashlight shining in his face to scare me. A week did not go by where he did not pull some stunt on me such as tricking me with joy buzzers or other pranks.

Fun Fact: The first video game to use stereo sound was *Sinistar* (1983) by Williams Electronics. It is an amazing game too!

A STRANGE ODYSSEY

This "handed-down" talent of course would come in handy later on and lead to one of my visits to Principal Nottingham, but more on that later. Knowing now what you have heard about my dad, you can imagine that it is next to impossible to fathom a trip of four hundred miles without him trying some kind of trick on me. If you are agreeing with me, then you will not be disappointed.

My dad began by insisting that I stay hydrated. The air conditioning was on so the car was cool, but he insisted I drink a bottle of water every hour. He also gave me several small beef jerky sticks that were salty. I probably should have expected that he was up to something, but my mind was awash in the thoughts of my new home and how desperate I was to fit in.

Fun Fact: Before becoming the popular character "Colonel Sherman Potter" on the sitcom M*A*S*H, actor Harry Morgan appeared on the show as zany General "Bartford Hamilton Steele".

CHAPTER ONE

Anyways, the salty snack ensured I drank a lot of water, more than he had anticipated. It was therefore not long before I told dad I needed to go to the bathroom; really badly. Now, if you have ever driven from Arizona to San Diego, you know there are miles and miles of nothing but highway and desert and rest stops are few and far between.

Dad pulled over on the side of the road and my mom pulled over a dozen yards away. Dad told me to go on the side of the road and the motorists would not see me because the car would be blocking their view. It seemed logical enough, so I got down to using the bathroom, aiming my pee at the remains of a tumbleweed.

I had not been too worried about someone seeing me go pee in public because there were

Fun Fact: The damsel-in-distress that Mario rescues in the original Donkey Kong is called Pauline.

not too many cars driving by. However, when my dad is pulling a fast one, the odds always seem to be in his favor. Several cars appeared on the horizon, zooming down this stretch of highway at a good eighty mile-per-hour clip.

As they approached, dad hit the gas gently and began rolling the car forward, leaving me without cover. At that moment, a half-dozen cars drove by and I was greeted with honks and wolf whistles.

The other, quite memorable comment was from a rather attractive girl that just may had been a marriage proposal, but I'm a bit too young for that. I tried not to look embarrassed, but instead shook my head; dad had gotten me again, *sigh*.

Now trips across the country can be stressful at the best of times, but they are worse in the heat, and even less-bearable when it involves

---

Embarrassing Fact: My roommates, when I was in my twenties, pulled the prank above on me.

multiple cars and the tension of moving. My mom did not find my dad's prank particularly funny and there was some shouting between our two cars on the freeway! I actually put an end to it by shouting "Will you both stop it? It is freaking hot out here and you are both acting like a couple of n00bs!"

Mom had no idea what that meant, but dad was a gamer and this comment he told me later had "cut me to the quick", whatever that meant. I got in the car and dad could not restrain himself from chuckling at his well-played prank. I smiled and agreed he got me good. However, my revenge was brewing; quite literally in my belly.

As I mentioned, dad had been sure to make me eat a lot of those spicy beef snacks. They were tiny, but at a quarter a piece, he had bought ten

---

Fun Fact: Jason Todd, the second Robin to partner with Batman was voted to be eliminated from the comic by fans, he was largely an unpopular Robin.

of them and I had eaten six. I ate the last four, saying I was hungry and the nearest restaurant was at least twenty or more miles away. Dad could hardly say no after prodding me to eat the first six, so he allowed me to eat them.

It was not ten minutes later when I released the first one. Now gas is never bad when it's your own, or at least it is not AS awful. However, there are exceptions to the rule; these were vile on an epic scale! If you've heard the term "Silent but deadly", these were indeed silent, but deadly was an understatement; try "Silent, but catastrophic"!

I would sit there and snicker. The first time, dad asked me what I was laughing at. Then he would sniff the air, make an unusual face, and say "Hugo, that is disgusting!" or something to that effect. Now he had a good sense of humor, so he laughed...at first.

Embarrassing Fact: My twin brother and I did a similar road trip and after eating a dozen small beef jerky sticks, I tormented him the same way as above during our journey.

CHAPTER ONE

After probably two or three dozen "bombs" in the car, he no longer thought they were quite so amusing...but I did. He began shouting "Hugo, that's enough!" Now I had read that (this is true, I really read this and the Internet never lies, right?) smelling passed gas actually can prevent cancer. So, with that in mind, when dad told me to stop, I'd say "Aren't you going to say thank you? After all dad, I'm trying to save your life."

"Yeah right Hugo. Seriously son, I think you may have a medical problem." He actually DID look like he meant that remark.

My response made it clear that I was not only unconcerned, but had no plans to stop barraging my dad with "Air Biscuits". "Dad, it may be medical, but I don't think it's a problem."

Fun Fact(?): There is actually a scientific theory that smelling someone's gas can help prevent cancer.

A STRANGE ODYSSEY

Even dad had to laugh at that. It was rare that I ever won a war of practical jokes with my dad, but for the remainder of the trip (which actually took ten hours), dad did not pull anything. We arrived at our new home at around seven o'clock in the evening with no further incidents (though I still mustered the occasional noxious fart).

So, I will sum up this part of my story by saying that in the long-running war of shenanigans between my dad and me; I declared myself the winner.

Fun Fact: The infamous "Steve Bartman" incident was likely an inspiration for the television crime drama *Law & Order* episode "Vendetta".

CHAPTER TWO

RIGHT INTO THE MESS

I had been so tired when we got to our new home that despite my anxiety at being in a new place, I had passed out asleep at shortly after eight o'clock and slept in until seven the next morning. I had half-expected dad to welcome me to my new home with a bucket of ice water (yes, he'd done this) or blasting the music on my clock radio.

Well, he must've either decided he had met his match in me, or was just being considerate of my need for rest; I woke up on my own and was able to rub my eyes and lounge about in bed for as long as I wanted.

Fun Fact: Are you afraid of the number thirteen? Then you have triskaidekaphobia.

RiGHT iNTO THE MESS

When my stomach began growling, I stood up, still wearing my pajamas and walked to the door and opened it. I had been wrong about my dad of course. It would have paid to be on my guard. I stepped across what I can only describe as a "trip wire" and a bucket above my head was tipped over.

Fortunately, it was not filled with ice water (after all, this was our new home, you don't want to soak the carpet). No, it was filled with packing peanuts, hundreds of them. Dad had upped his game as he stood there with his Smartphone, video recording the whole event. I had no doubt that someday I would bring a date over and this would be playing on the television as I led her into the living room.

I suppose I should comment that my dad and mom are good people and they do love me very

Shameless Book Plug: Marie Andreas' *The Lost Ancients* and *The Asarlaí Wars* series. For High School-age readers and older.

much. It is just that my dad, even at the age of thirty-four is trying to deny the fast-approaching scourge of becoming old and does this by acting my age instead of his. Hey, it's never dull with him around, right?

Anyways, I ate breakfast; a nourishing meal of bacon, hash browns, scrambled eggs and toast. I have a unique way of enjoying this meal. I eat the eggs with a fork after putting a ton of pepper on it. Then I take the hash browns and bacon and put it between the slices of toast and eat it like a sandwich. Sound weird? Maybe, but it is epic!

As I was cleaning my dishes dad walked in carrying a brand-new baseball glove and a Seattle Seahawks baseball cap. "Here ya go sport!" I winced. I love baseball and I share my dad's love of the Seahawks (my grandfather, who passed years before I was born was from

---

Embarrassing Fact: I do actually enjoy making this sandwich for breakfast, even as unhealthy as it is.

RiGHT iNTo THE MESS

Seattle), but whatever surprise this was had prank written all over it. As it turned out, I was wrong, but it was a typical dad plan nonetheless, so I was right to wince. "I got these for you the other day as a surprise. I signed you up for Little League."

Now I love baseball, so this should've made me smile. However, here I was, brand new in the city less than one day and already I'm getting right into the mess of things. I slept well, but my dreams were of the worries of making new friends and here I was being thrust onto a baseball team.

"Hey bud, they are practicing today in about two hours. Why don't you take a shower, get

---

Fun Fact: An old prank is an envelope with the label "Rattlesnake eggs". Don't fall for it; rattlesnakes do not lay eggs.

dressed, and we'll get there early so you can warm up before it starts." He handed the glove to me. "Here, try it on."

Dad always said "Fool me once, shame on you, fool me twice, shame on me." I took the glove from him and shook it upside down. The tiny joy buzzer dropped out of the pocket where my index finger would've gone.

I smiled at my dad's disappointment. "Too predictable, n00b." I said and he laughed.

"It was worth a try. Good heads-up." He patted my head and then walked to the sink to begin cleaning the dishes.

I jumped in the shower and noticed for the first time, I was getting a little stubble on my lip and chin. Odd, it had not been there yesterday, but it was there. I looked in the cabinet and dad had unpacked his shaving cream and razor. I had never shaved before, but I had seen him do it; how hard could it be?

Fun Fact: n00b is a gaming term, often derogatory for a novice or newcomer.

RiGHT iNTO THE MESS

I lathered up as I had seen dad do hundreds of times and soon I was covered from the bottom of my neck to just below my eyes with shaving cream.

I looked in the mirror and recognized a fact; I looked ridiculous. Dad just happened to be walking by and of course he found this alternately hilarious and frightening. I guess it was luck that he caught me just as I was about to make my first swipe.

Needless to say, I would need to wait until another day for my clean close shave. Then again, dad made it sound like he had saved me from one as well.

I ONCE CAUGHT A FISH THIS BIG!

Fun Fact: The story above reflects my first time shaving. I did not cut myself, but I made one doozy of a mess! Oh, and I once caught a 26-inch Largemouth Bass.

CHAPTER THREE

A PITCH FOR THE ANGELS

Zebras cannot change their stripes, or so they say. No matter what clothes I put on, I could not change how frightened I was about the drive over to the ballpark. I dressed in my "Task Force: Gaea" t-shirt, my Seahawks hat, and a pair of baseball pants that were only two lengths too big for me now. I looked like a rube as my dad would have said were he insensitive, but I knew the kids at the field would say I looked like an utter n00b; hey it rhymes at least.

Dad drove me to the game. Mom wanted to go, but she was not feeling all that good and

---

Fun Fact: The title "A Pitch for the Angels" is a nod to one of my favorite *Twilight Zone* episodes.

decided instead to lie down. We listened to a band from Finland called "Poets of the Fall" and I found their music to be fun and it got me in a pumped-up mood for baseball.

"Dad," I asked. "do you think I will get a chance to pitch?"

"Well I spoke to the manager before we left Arizona yesterday. I told him you were a great hitter and played a solid outfield, but that you had been practicing pitching and had an evolving curveball. He promised he would let you throw a few pitches today."

"Thanks dad, I am not sure if I am any good, but I hope I can find out."

"Well, Hugo, I am no judge of velocity; after all, we have no radar gun. However, you do throw strikes and that tells me you at least have a shot."

Fun Fact: The Split-Finger Fastball, despite the name, is considered an off-speed pitch.

CHAPTER THREE

We did not say much the rest of the way there. Dad turned right and drove up a serpentine drive and we found ourselves in a parking lot that sat between two baseball fields, a small snack bar building off to the right.

Dad pointed to a stocky man with a beard who was about average height. He had a pierced nose and another one above his left eyebrow that I admit kind of worried me. Dad di not notice and simply said "That's Bob, the manager of your team, the Angels."

Fun Fact: Bob is loosely based on my best friend (and fellow Seahawks fan, Bob Vehon).

A PITCH FOR THE ANGELS

I stepped out nervously and dad handed me my glove, my cleats, and somewhat embarrassingly, an athletic supporter and a cup. "Dad, couldn't you have given me these before we left?"

He shrugged and then said "At least I got you this." He handed me a ball cap that had the team logo. "The first step towards fitting in on your new team."

I smiled and dashed off to the bathroom to put my "extra clothing' on while dad talked to "Coach Bob" as he wished to be called. I came out and was introduced to coaches Steve and Randy. Steve handled the pitchers, Randy handled the outfielders. I supposed that Bob managed the team AND handled the infielders, but I knew I would find out.

Bob shook my hand and I was relieved to find out it was not a "crush the cartilage" handshake.

Fun Fact: Dad's shirt above has a pixel drawing I did of Daryl from the television show *The Walking Dead*.

It was firm, but polite. I smiled as he had changed his Angels hat for a Seahawks hat...Go Hawks! I was still nervous, but still, Bob seemed nice enough and his welcome to the team was genuine.

"So, your dad says you are a good hitter and outfielder, but want to pitch huh?"

"Yes sir." I said timidly.

The players around me laughed. Bob smiled and said "You can call me sir if you make an error, until then, I am Coach Bob, ya got me?"

"Yes si....er Coach Bob."

"Alright. Your dad did not know I moved the practice up an hour early, so you go ahead and stretch out while the boys take the field. Once you are ready, you come over and take the mound and we'll see what you got."

Fun Fact: There was a Japanese version of *Spider-Man* on television in the 1970s; it was called *Supaidaman*.

A PITCH FOR THE ANGELS

Dad patted me on the shoulder and walked me off to the side where he ran me through some stretching exercises he used when playing softball. I think it is important to mention that dad is one epic softball player. He is tall and extremely skinny, so he does not look like a hitter, but he can really hit the ball with power. The secret he said is contact and bat speed; and boy does he have it. It remained to be seen if I really had it.

DAD PLAYING SOFTBALL

I had never really played baseball before except taking pitches at the local batting cages and live throws from dad. I would go to the park and practice fielding, but I was a bit of a "lone wolf" so joining a team now was a big first for me. I was so nervous, I thought I would lose my breakfast, but I kept it in.

Fun Fact: I am a diehard softball player and like Hugo's dad, can hit for power despite being skinny.

CHAPTER THREE

I finally took the field and stood on the mound. At least this was familiar. Dad had erected a mound at the correct distance and height in our backyard in our old home and so pitching to a catcher here was not much different. A member of the team named Terrell was wearing the gear and crouched at the plate.

"Ok, let's see it Hugo." Coach Bob said,

I wound up, raising both arms above my head and then coming forward, released my hardest fastball. It was at this moment I realized I had stretched out, but had thrown no warm-up pitches and this one bounced in the dirt about six feet before the plate.

I had expected to hear laughter, but the other players were doing a variety of drills and Terrell seemed more displeased than amused.

"Hey, throw some soft tosses until you feel ready." Coach Steve said.

Fun Fact: I mention a tsunami or at least one happens in every one of my books. We'll see where it turns up in this book.

A PITCH FOR THE ANGELS

So, Terrell stood and I played a short game of catch. Dad had originally planned to do this with me, but again, we did not get to practice early and dad did not want to interfere. Luckily Terrell was patient with me. After maybe about twenty throws back and forth, I nodded and he went back into the crouch.

Coach Steve commented "Wind up with your arms to your chest, not over your head. Players can steal bases during the windup and this will save you a half-second."

I was fine with this, having practiced with a variety of windups, but the over-the-head one was my favorite. Oh well. Anyways, I wound up as Coach Steve suggested and uncorked my best fastball. It zoomed right down the middle of the plate and I heard a loud "Whap!" noise to accompany it.

Fun Fact: When I was in Little League, the over-the-head windup was popular.

"Good pitch Hugo. Now let's see some velocity."

"Uh" I said, not knowing what to say. Coach Bob was not picking on me; he literally did not believe my fastball was overpowering. Sadly, that was my best one. I uncorked another one, throwing as much muscle and weight into it as I could.

"Whap!" Bob came over. "Hugo, level with me, is that your best fastball?"

"Yes Coach Bob, I gave that one all I had. Was it bad?"

"Son, you nailed the strike zone both times, but the pitch itself was not particularly fast, nor did it have movement. In a word, it was flat. I am afraid unless you have some wicked breaking stuff, you won't do well as a pitcher."

"I can throw a curve." I answered somewhat lamely.

Was Marty McFly a bee? Not all bees are hard workers, there are bees that are lazy and avoid work. Yep, there are "slacker" bees!

A PITCH FOR THE ANGELS

Bob nodded and pointed at Terrell to crouch back down. I threw a dozen of my best curveballs and a few more fastballs, dreading what his final evaluation of my pitching ability would be. It would not be too long before I found out.

Fun Fact: Wet a piece of used spaghetti and place it on a sleeping person's lips. It will feel like a worm when they wake up.

CHAPTER FOUR

OPENING DAY

The drive home later was one of disappointment. Dad spent much of it consoling me and reminding me that I had done well overall. That much was true, but not where it really mattered to me.

After probably thirty pitches when Coaches Bob and Steve were certain my arm was loose, they pulled me aside. Well, I can't remember exactly what they said, but in a nutshell, I had excellent control; after all, I threw pretty much every pitch for strikes. However, my fastball was not adequate to blow a batter away and my curve hung one-half of the time.

I did not mind this so much, but Coach Randy brought in third baseman Brad Edmunds who proceeded to pulverize nine out of ten of my pitches, several of them over the fence and into

Fun Fact: The Bad News Bears (the original one anyways) is widely considered one of the best baseball movies of all time.

the canyon beyond. I did manage to make him swing and miss at ONE of my pitches though.

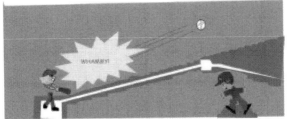

Coach Bob explained that Denny Marquis and Stan Richards had pretty much locked up the pitching spots, so there was little room for me on the mound. As you might guess, I was disappointed, but managed to give them a smile and a nod as I headed out to center field.

I did impress all three coaches as I showed my good speed and instincts out there. I ran all over the place, diving for fly balls and the only thing I did not impress with was my arm. I guess my throwing arm really was not that good.

I got into the batter's box and while I was not as powerful as Brad Edmunds, I was not far behind. I proudly walloped four pitches over the fence, showed that I could lay off bad pitches, and even put a dent in the scoreboard off of one of Denny Marquis' best fastballs.

Fun Fact: Denny Marquis mentioned above is a nod to former major league pitcher Jason Marquis who I was a fan of.

CHAPTER FOUR

The team had an "everyone makes the team" policy, but Coach Bob told me I made it on my merit and would be the starting Center Fielder tomorrow at ten o'clock in the morning. I guessed that was something and I knew my moping was a bit immature, but what do you expect from an eleven-year-old?

I had at least made several friends. A pair of brothers named Marcus and Liam (who were Twelve and Eleven respectively and played left field and right field respectively) helped me fill out a strong defensive trio in the outfield. They also were a pair of speedy runners and it looked like Marcus would bat first, Liam second, me third, and Brad fourth. For the life of me I could not remember the rest of the lineup.

Mom was still not feeling all that great, complaining that she was nauseous. Dad took me to "Six Dudes", a burger place that was really

---

Fun Fact: Marcus and Liam are the sons of my good friends Tom and Sandra.

popular. Each table had a small video game console and a selection of movies and it only cost one dollar to use. Dad and I watched the original "Bad News Bears" movie, which seemed in the spirit of the day's events and tomorrow's game.

We had a fun meal and dad reminded me of how proud he was of me a dozen times which made me feel good and helped me forget my failure as a pitcher. I came home and mom was in bed and dad asked me to take a shower and brush my teeth and put myself to bed; I had a big day ahead of me.

I did not sleep very well that evening. I was worried that I would disgrace the team and be an outcast and be asked to quit. I also wondered

---

Baseball Fact: There are technically seven ways for a runner to get on base without getting a hit.

if I would awaken in the morning to my dad yelling "Attack of the wild dogs!" or some such joke to get me up in a hurry.

Mom was feeling better the next morning, though she did not have much of an appetite. They both assured me she was ok and that was one thing; they never lied to me. That concern removed, I ate up, again with what I had termed my "Breakfast Sandwich Supreme" which made dad laugh and my mom nearly turn green.

"Hurry up pal, those home runs won't hit themselves." Dad said.

I bitterly replied "They will if I am pitching."

"Now cut that out Hugo!" Dad sounded mad, but his expression was in more of an understanding bent. "If you want to pitch, you'll just have to work harder, right?"

"I guess. Instead I'll just make sure their pitchers look bad."

Fun Fact: On many pages (like this one), I hide (in plain sight) the titles of my friend's books for fun.

OPENING DAY

"That's the spirit! Now get dressed and let's hit the field!"

I arrived at the field and posed for team pictures with Marcus and Liam next to me. I found out that they also would be attending Tom Harkin Middle School with me tomorrow. Marcus would be starting the seventh grade and this was his second year there and Liam would be in the sixth grade with me. It was reassuring that I would have a few friends to keep me company and ensure I was not a total n00b at school.

There was one thing I noticed during the pictures that was somewhat suspicious. Denny Marquis and Stan Richards were not there for them. Were they each warming up for the game? That made no sense! I mean after all, only one of them would pitch the game, unless

---

Fun Fact: Tom Harkin is a retired Senator from the state of Iowa. I am a huge fan of his.

the other one would be a reliever. No, that made no sense, since a reliever would not warm up so early.

Oh well, I thought, it was not my concern. I had gotten myself excited to be part of a trio of all-star quality outfielders with my new pals Marcus and Liam and even pitching did not seem like such a big deal to me. I found that I was not really even disappointed about not pitching and the thought of it no longer excited me.

At least that is what I thought until Coach Bob walked up to the three of us and dropped a bombshell on me.

Fun Fact: By weight, the Green Anaconda is the largest snake in the world. It is found in the South American rainforests.

CHAPTER FIVE

Mayhem on the Mound

Coach Bob's face looked grave; well, desperate was more like it. Coaches Steve and Randy were with him and they looked like they were about to tell me that a disaster had just happened, like maybe Independence Day Three was being made, or worse (no, nothing could be worse than that).

"Son, you are not going to believe this, but Stan Richards and Denny Marquis both came down with a stomach bug." He looked on the

---

Fun Fact: Sadly, the second *Independence Day* movie "Resurgence" is considered one of the worst sequels ever. I would see another sequel as a nightmare.

verge of tears. "I'm afraid I'm going to need you to step up to the mound and pitch."

It is funny, but yesterday it was all I wanted in the world. However, after watching Brad launch several home runs off of my best pitches; some of which I doubt have landed yet, being thrust into this job was the last thing I wanted. Yesterday I was mildly worried that I would puke, and now I practically ran to the bathroom. Uh, I did not remember eating THAT! Ugh!

I came out and was met by Marcus and Liam and another kid by the name of Bryson. Bryson, it turned out had not been at the practice yesterday; he'd apparently been suffering the same stomach bug that had felled Denny and Stan.

(Left to Right: Liam, Marcus, Bryson, and Hugo)

Fun Fact: Bryson is the son of a friend of mine and fellow author Terra James.

CHAPTER FIVE

"I know how you feel, I don't remember throwing up so much since I saw *The Bachelor*".

I laughed, this new friend was funny and he made my stomach feel better and helped me relax. The four of us walked onto the field where I found out there was no rest for the wicked; we were the home team, so I was sent directly to the mound.

I looked around and memorized the names of my teammates. Terrell was catching, Jesus Diaz was at first base, Jimmy Berner was playing second base, Schuyler "Mac" Arthur was at shortstop, Brad was at third. In the outfield, Marcus and Liam were at left and right field, and Kristoffer Davies was in my place at center field.

Coach Bob had a motivational speech prepared for me. Ok, it was not really a motivational

---

Fun Fact: Iguanas not only sneeze, they sneeze more than any animal on Earth (including people).

speech per se. No, he wanted me to know that Brad Helms, the opposing manager was a jerk and more than anything he was depending on me to pitch the game of my life and help beat these guys. How delightfully helpful; especially after I had learned yesterday that I was an awful pitcher.

Well, there was no stalling now. Mitchell Snide came up to the plate. Yes, that really was his last name and it perfectly described his personality. The only thing bigger than his mouth was his nose, which was the size of a butter knife.

"Hey, new kid, Arizona huh? When they play your song backwards, you can listen to how badly we beat you!"

MITCHELL SNIDE

I had nothing to lose, so I decided to respond in kind. "Well, good thing this game ain't a movie,

Fun Fact: Snide is a player for the "New York Apples" in the *Turbografx-16* game *World Class Baseball*. This is a nod to him, one of my favorite players in the game.

you couldn't see it unless they played it on your nose...which is a double-wide screen!"

Snide gave me a look that was...well...snide. He got into a batting crouch in the batter's box. I decided to give them the slow pitches they expected, but not where they wanted them. My first pitch I threw at least a foot outside.

Snide swung and missed. Then he did it again, and again. Three fastballs, three swings, and three strikes. Well, it technically was six strikes if you count his nose, but now I was just being mean.

The next batter, Lonnie Egan came to the plate. I could see he was not as short-sighted as Snide. This time I went to my curve. I hung it (not intentionally, my curves just are not that good), but located them on the inside and outside corners, just far enough out. On the third pitch, he hammered it...straight up into the air.

Fun Fact: *Star Trek* has had over 125 videos games based on or inspired by it made.

MAYHEM ON THE MOUND

Brad must not have liked Lonnie too much. He stood there at first and mimicked eating a sandwich while waiting for the ball to drop into my glove. Hilarious!

The next batter, John Brick was possibly the biggest eleven or twelve-year-old I had seen. I went back to the pattern I used with Snide for the first two pitches and he swung and missed. Then I surprised him by doing the least clever thing ever; I threw a fastball right over the plate! Nine pitches, nine strikes, three outs.

Marcus and Liam both reached base on bunt singles and I sadly did not hit well, flying out to mid-left field. Brad however doubled off of the wall and scored them both before the inning ended.

Fun Fact: Well, not for cavemen. A theory suggests that the eruption of the Toba "supervolcano" nearly wiped them out 70,000 years ago.

CHAPTER FIVE

For four more innings I pitched that way. I had a nearly-perfect game with the exception of one walk and that was erased with a double-play on a line drive to Jesus who then tagged first. I had a bit of a blip in the fourth when I walked the fourth, fifth, and sixth batter in the order. It had become clear my strategy had failed.

I had needed to dig deep. Brad walked over to the mound and began shouting at me.

"You are a disgrace! Can't you throw one strike anymore? You are embarrassing the team!" He shoved me and then returned to his position.

I stood just behind the mound and looked over angrily at Marty Joyce who was the first walk I had issued. He decided he would give Brad some lip too.

"Hey, did you want to yell at our pitcher, Ernie Kawa if he walks one of you guys too?"

Historical Fact: The American Revolutionary War actually began in 1775

MAYHEM ON THE MOUND

"Naw, but I think your teammates are going to yell at you."

"Oh, why is that Brad?" He said this smugly.

"Because you're out n00b!" he said this laughing as he tagged Marty with the ball.

Brad had used his shove of me as an opportunity to take the ball from my glove. I had thought he was really mad, but then realized he had the ball and I now stood there waiting for him to return it, which he now did.

I whispered "Why didn't you tell me you were doing the hidden ball trick when you shoved me? I thought you really hated me for a second."

Brad smiled back at me "I was trying to really sell it, and we did. By the way, you are doing great, we're proud of you Hugo, now go get 'em." With that, he ran back to third base.

Fun Fact: I once "faked" a Hidden Ball Trick. The runner, believing he was out, walked towards the dugout; our pitcher then ran over and tagged him out for real.

CHAPTER FIVE

With one out, I managed to get the next batter to hit a ground ball to Brad, but he bobbled it and the bases were loaded again.

My arm felt like spaghetti and even though the eighth and ninth batters were due up, I was worried. I decided to give it my all and just trust in myself. I threw a fastball down the middle and he popped up. Two outs, followed by a third when I struck out their pitcher Ernie Kawa gawking at a pitch that was not really a strike, but apparently the umpire thought was close enough.

I had a no-hitter so far, and my dad was proud. Marcus came over and gave me a fist-bump also. However, the sixth inning was where my both my true prowess and all-too-real inadequacies were exposed.

Fun Fact: During an interview, Washington Nationals pitcher Gio Gonzalez worked the word "Meow" in eleven times while playing the "Cat Game".

CHAPTER SIX

They call me "The Babe"

The score was still 2-0 in our favor. I had hit a triple in my second at-bat, but had not scored; Brad had lined out to end the inning. Marcus and Liam had grounded out to the shortstop whose throw had beaten them by an eyelash at first; boy were these two fast! They would lead off the bottom of the sixth, but that would only happen if I blew the lead and I had no plan to do so.

Sadly, my plans and what really happened were not in complete sync with one another. Snide hit a single off of me that practically knocked me off of my feet! He then stole second. Egan then singled, scoring Snide.

Fun Fact: The title of this chapter is based on the fact that Babe Ruth was originally a power-hitting pitcher.

THEY CALL ME "THE BABE"

There were still no outs. Brick then launched a home run that probably put a hole in the Big Dipper's cup. I had gone from a no-hitter to being behind 3-2; I had let my team, Coach Bob, and my dad down.

There were still no outs and despite my success, they had a rather impressive group of hitters. Even Ernie Kawa, their pitcher had a pretty wicked swing. Coach Bob came out to me and I thought he would be mad, but his expression was unreadable.

"Hey kid, how you holding up?"

"Not good sir, I blew it!"

"Are you kidding? This team usually scores nine or ten runs per game. THIS is actually a victory for me."

Baseball Fact: An early version of the pickoff play called "Soaking" allowed the pitcher to hit the runner with the ball. If it hit the runner, he was out.

CHAPTER SIX

"Well, let's put it this way coach, my arm is as weak as a kitten. Do you have anyone else?"

Coach Bob looked over towards Bryson. "Well, he's been sick and he's not likely one hundred percent, but Bryson there has a cannon arm. I've been grooming him to be the closer."

"Well, he can't be in any worse shape than I'm in. I'm not a quitter coach, but if I stay in, I'll hurt the team."

He nodded and turned towards the bench. "Bryson! Get over here!"

Bryson had looked a bit sad, not expecting to play. The rule was that everyone played, but because he had been sick, Coach Bob had likely planned to let him pinch hit or play first base for the last out. Now he was getting a chance to pitch. If he had been sick, he sure looked vibrant now. He ran and I mean he RAN to the mound.

Fun Fact: Bat guano (poop) is used in antibiotics.

THEY CALL ME "THE BABE"

"Ok Bryson, I've only got three words to say to you son; GO GET `EM!" He tossed Bryson the ball and then said to me "Go take Kristoffer's place in Center, he's been limping since that diving catch last inning and besides I don't want to lose your bat when we're up after Bryson gets us out of this mess."

I winked at Bryson as I walked by him and he said nothing, but smiled at me. I ran out and Kristoffer showed he was a good sport, giving me a high-five as we passed and said "Good pitching!" to me. I might not have done as well as I had thought, but I had indeed pitched the game of my life. Now if only we could win.

Bryson stood at the mound and the fourth, fifth, and sixth batters looked to continue their torrid onslaught against us. However, much like

---

Fun Fact: Kristoffer is the son of a friend of mine and is also believed to be the world's youngest hacker.

my plan to pitch a no-hitter, their plan to expand upon their lead did not bear out. Bryson threw nine fastballs and got nine swinging strikes to get us out of the inning.

We all mobbed Bryson as if he had just won the World Series and in a way, his accomplishment was just as important. I mean he had gotten us out of a jam and we had a chance to win. Now we just needed to follow through.

Marcus did not swing the bat once. He drew a walk on four straight pitches. Liam got ahold of one and took it to the center field fence. He had not struck me as a batter with power, but he'd really nailed this one. However, Egan made a diving catch to get Liam out. Marcus however had tagged up from first and reached second base.

Baseball Fact: Striking out the side on nine pitches is incredibly rare. As a Padres fan, I am glad to say Brian Lawrence did it for us on 06/12/2002.

THEY CALL ME "THE BABE"

There was one out and a runner in scoring position. If I could whack a single, I could at least tie the game and that would be enough for us. Well, we would be content, but I wanted to win.

I walked up to the plate with the chance to be a hero or a goat" as the expression goes and hoped I would be the former.

Ernie Kawa leered at me from the mound. "You're going to strike out on three pitches and embarrass your team further."

"I doubt it. The strongest thing you have left is your breath!"

Now I normally do not care for trash-talking. My dad and mom raised me better than that. However, they had been talking that way to me

---

Fun Fact: Mel Blanc, the voice of *Bugs Bunny* actually ate carrots while voicing the character. Allegedly, he hated carrots too.

throughout the whole game and it had given me an idea.

Between innings, Brad had told me Ernie liked to plunk people with fastballs; it made them reluctant to crowd the plate later in the game. I suspected if I razzed him enough, he would throw inside at me, maybe even at my head.

That is just what he did and it was the biggest mistake he ever made. Just before he released the ball, I stepped a couple of inches back from the plate, while staying inside the batter's box. Then I opened my stance and turned towards left field and swung.

The ball had been coming at my head, but now was just a tad inside, which was where the sweet spot of my bat met it as well. My bat spun around with me; the ball carried a good ten feet over the left field fence for a game-winning home run.

Fun Fact: Sad, but true, I used to play with a pitcher who loved to drill people with pitches. Needless to say, he will remain nameless.

THEY CALL ME "THE BABE"

I heard Coach Bob the loudest, shouting "Way to go Hugo! Way to go Angels!" He could not resist shouting over at Brad Helms "Where's your big mouth now Brad?" Of course, Brad, the player on our team did a double-take, but then laughed. I laughed too as Coach Bob was wearing his Seahawks hat instead of his Angels hat.

The shaking of hands by the players after the game had me nervous. I half-expected one of them to punch me in the face. This did not happen. I was surprised that Snide and Kawa both presented a fist instead of a hand and gave me a fist bump, both of them saying "Mad props, respect."

I had not exactly played the way I expected, but I would not have exchanged this experience for any other.

Baseball Fact: The fastest baseball game in history lasted less than an hour!

PART II
JUST ANOTHER MANIC MONDAY

Fun Fact: The title above is a reference to a song by the *Bangles*.

CHAPTER SEVEN
THE FIRST DAY

There was a ton of celebration after the game. Dad took me to join the rest of the team at "The Hat", a pizza place that catered to youth sports teams. It is a remarkable place that offers baskets of shelled peanuts for fifty cents, plays old movies and cartoons on an original projector, and has pinball and video games from an era that belongs to my dad's childhood.

I joined Marcus, Liam, and Bryson at an arcade cabinet where we played a game of *Gauntlet*. I chose the Valkyrie, Bryson the Warrior, Marcus the Wizard, and Liam the Elf. The four of us played it for quite some time on just a handful of quarters.

Fun Fact: The original game Gauntlet was released in 1985 and has numerous remakes. It is a true classic!

THE FiRST DAY

Our pizza was done and I met the parents of my new friends and we made indefinite plans to visit one another at our respective houses and I was very excited about this. It was a really good time. Mitchell Snide and Ernie Kawa came over and let me know there were no hard feelings; Coach Helms had taught and instructed them to talk trash, it was part of the game, or so they were told.

Well, all good things must come to an end and we all had to prepare for school the next day. I was pretty sure that the staff at The Hat was happy to see us go after spending close to six hours in there and spending very little money. I said goodbye to Bryson, Liam, and Marcus, and gave a wave to Ernie and Mitchell. Then I hopped into dad's car and headed home.

Mom I saw was lying in bed. I was worried as she looked pale and was obviously not feeling

---

Fun Fact: *Gauntlet* the arcade game had some controversy due to similar game called *Dandy* released earlier in 1983. There was even a lawsuit involved.

well. Again, her and dad assured me she was fine; it was just a little nausea. I promised them I would not worry, and again, since they had never lied to me, I put it out of my mind.

I was actually somewhat hungry, so I cooked myself a couple of hamburgers and French fries for dinner. After eating, I headed up to the upstairs bathroom and took a shower. Even though it was a bit early, I dressed in my pajamas and retired to my room where I opened my closet and from a large cardboard box, withdrew a pair of comic books.

I finished reading them and began feeling sleepy, so I got up, brushed my teeth, and crawled into bed and closed my eyes. I had not

Fun Fact: The first comic book I ever bought was *The Avengers* # 220 (Printed 1982). *Drax the Destroyer* who is in the *Guardians of the Galaxy* movies dies in this issue.

THE FiRST DAY

slept well the night before because I was nervous. I was equally anxious about the first day of school, but I was also exhausted and sleep claimed me pretty quickly.

The next morning I awoke and got dressed in a pair of jeans and a new jacket that mom must have laid out for me. She always wanted me to look good, especially for the first day of school. I walked downstairs and dad had left already for his new job. Mom was still in her pajamas, but had made breakfast; yes, my usual "Breakfast Sandwich Supreme."

Mom was in better health this morning, bounding about with her old energy. She peppered me with questions about what elective I would take

Fun Fact: In at least one version of King's Quest IV, typing "BEAM ME" after defeating the villain, takes your character into a spaceship where you meet the game's programmers.

for school. I really had no idea, but I had only one to select from and this school had quite a selection. I thoughtfully told her I would consider my options and let her know.

Mom originally had planned to drive me, but I elected to walk. It was only about one mile away and Marcus and Liam it turned out lived only a few blocks away. I saw them walking by, so I kissed mom goodbye and rushed out to meet them.

They greeted me and we journeyed together. Marcus told me Tom Harkin Middle School was not all that bad, though they did have a few bullies. I'd not had to deal with them at my old school in Arizona, but I was confident I would be fine. I was tall, athletic, and my Uncle Danny who was a Marine taught me a few dozen moves I could use to defend myself. However, I told

Fun Fact: The movie *The Last Starfighter* purchased the rights to the name *Starfighter* from game company *Adventure International*.

myself I would never need to fight and would avoid trouble if possible.

We got to the school and there we were forced to split up. Liam and Marcus were in a different "letter" section based on last names. We had not discussed trying to be in classes together and Marcus is a year older than me, so it was unlikely I would share too many with him.

I got in line and saw a few familiar faces around me from yesterday's game. Ernie Kawa, John Brick, and Mitchell Snide were around and they each gave me a friendly nod. Bryson, I saw was in a line two sections over from me and I smiled at him as he was surrounded by a few other students who wanted details of his perfect inning yesterday; he deserved it.

I chose Journalism as my elective as the Middle School had a monthly paper and I

Fun Fact: My mother does not like video games, but she did play *Kangaroo* (1982) once. Her kangaroo died quickly.

thought it would be fun. It would be my second period class. I saw that I had basic science for first period and this also sounded like fun.

I saw that Liam was heading towards the same classroom, so I was excited that my first class at my new school would be with a good friend. However, my excitement died down as I viewed who my teacher was. Staring down at me and Liam, his face practically dripping with hatred...was Brad Helms, coach of yesterday's opposing baseball team!

Fun Fact: Pterodactyls are not classified as dinosaurs; they were actually flying reptiles.

CHAPTER EIGHT
FIRST PERIOD

If I could have picked the worst possible scenario, Brad Helms being one of my teachers certainly was it! He scowled at me with his yellow eyes. OK, they weren't yellow, but they had the look of a lion about to bring down an antelope. To use another animal analogy, I fully expected that like a pack of hyenas on a zebra, he'd keep nipping away at my heels until I was brought down.

I looked and did not see that any members of his baseball team were in the class and only Liam was here in the class with me from my team. Well, at least I had a friend and would not have to face him alone.

Fun Fact: The planet Pluto is one-third water.

FiRST PERiOD

I hoped that he would be like a regular teacher and not take out his humiliating loss because of my surprisingly-good pitching and wicked swing on me, but would accept that every game has a winner and a loser and he happened to be a loser yesterday. Somehow by the look in his eyes, I could tell that my hopes were not going to come true.

"Well, well, we have a couple of baseball heroes here today." Yikes, this did not sound good. "I do think that we are going to have a fun school year here in first period, don't you Hugo?"

I gulped. "Yes...uh...yes sir." I had hoped to be defiant, but I admit I was quite terrified of him. I mean his teeth had four sharp canines and they were yellowed, like a man who had drank

---

Fun Fact: Well, not really fun. Brad Helms is based on an actual coach from my Little League years.

tea and chewed tobacco since he was in the womb! I swore for a second he had horns and I almost looked for a pitchfork!

His breath smelled like shoe polish mixed with bad coffee and his eyes were not yellow as I said, but were an unhealthy pale green color. A precursor to the Zombie Apocalypse, maybe? I had to remain calm. Maybe I could ask to be switched to a different science class and so could Liam? Speaking of Liam, he had waited until Mr. Helms turned around and made several faces at him.

The class snickered and he whirled his head around, but could not see why the class laughed. Truthfully though, I bet he had a sixth sense and knew it was either Liam or me. I also

---

Parental Lecture: Tobacco is not only gross, it is very bad for you in so many ways. Please do not smoke or chew tobacco.

FiRST PERiOD

thought for a second he had a forked tail, but it was probably just my imagination.

"So class, at least a couple of you know I coach a baseball team and I believe it is best to get the first pitch out of the way. So, we are going to do a little science experiment today just to get you all introduced to Middle School science.

He went over to a large stand-up locker and began pulling out plastic bottles of ketchup. I had no idea what experiment this would be, but the look on his face certainly did not bode well, at least not for me. He began handing out the bottles, one to each student and then yelled "Do not do anything with them yet!"

Science Fact: Yes, you can indeed clean pennies with ketchup, though of course you then need to clean up the mess afterwards.

CHAPTER EIGHT

He managed to give each one out and then went to a jar full of pennies. "We are going to use this ketchup to clean them. It is a simple experiment, but since you are all new to science, we need to start simple."

Soon we all had pennies and a bottle of ketchup. He walked over to his desk and then began handing out paper plates. "Put the penny on the middle of the plates as soon as you get them please."

I watched as each student did so and I complied as well. Soon we all had ketchup bottles, a penny each, and a paper plate beneath them. The pennies all looked a bit old and rusted, which may have been the point here.

Shameless Book(s) Plug: *The Treemakers Trilogy* by Christina L. Rozelle

FiRST PERiOD

"OK, so everyone, eyes on me." He said in a commanding tone.   He held up the bottle of ketchup.

There are times in a person's life, even one as young as mine where you have those little voices in your head. They are quiet and we often ignore them, but they are actually warnings from our brain saying "Look out, this will not end well." I either did not hear the voice at this time, or ignored it. I would learn to regret not paying attention to it this day.

"Now, before you pour the ketchup onto the plate, you need to shake the bottle." Did I see him grin expectantly?

Well, I did as he said and the lid suddenly popped open and ketchup began spraying into my face.

Fun Fact: Yes, there is a trick where you can put baking soda into a ketchup bottle and shaking it will make it spray everywhere. No, I do not want you to try it.

CHAPTER EIGHT

It was thin and more of a liquid form than the thick ketchup that normally comes out of the bottle. My face was covered in it and it began dripping onto the desk and the plate (the penny too, so at least it would be clean).

The class laughed at me, except for Liam who had dashed over to the wall near the door and grabbed several paper towels. He began wiping my face and the table, trying to help clean up the mess. My vision was clear, but my ears were echoing with the laughter of the students...and that of Mr. Helms whose voice was even louder than the class; yes, he was laughing at me!

I looked down and Liam had gotten much of it cleaned up and he was leaving to get more towels. My shirt looked like the scene from a horror movie, with ketchup splattered all over

Baseball Fact: The 1916 Philadelphia Athletics had a record of 36 wins and 117 losses for a modern baseball worst win/loss percentage of .235.

it. I could still feel it on my face and my hair. I of course could run to the sink and clean it, but my shirt would be stained for the rest of the day, if not ruined.

"Mr. Finley, I did not tell you to shake the bottle with all of your might. Perhaps that lucky home run you hit yesterday got you thinking you were superhuman?"

I exploded, more so than the ketchup bottle had. "You did this! You intentionally gave me a ketchup bottle with baking soda in it to pay me back for making you look like a loser yesterday!"

"First of all Mr. Finley, SAY it don't SPRAY it. Second of all, I will NOT be talked to like that!

Fun Fact: The 1983 laserdisc video game *Dragon's Lair* had a continuity error. While hero Dirk the Daring chased after his sword, the animation also showed it at his side in his scabbard.

I am a teacher and you hardly made anyone but yourself look bad yesterday."

I am not sure how **I** looked bad yesterday, but he did not give me a chance to dwell on it. "I think you need to leave this room and visit the principal."

I stood up, wordlessly and walked over to the sink to at least clean off a bit more of the ketchup from my face and clothes.

"No, Mr. Finley, you will go now! You can clean yourself up after you speak to Principal Nottingham!" Fighting back angry tears, I walked out of the classroom.

Fun Fact: Fun Fact: When coming up with the concept for Mr. Helms, I wanted someone who looked mean. To that end, I based his look on actor R. Lee Ermey, who is a former drill instructor.

CHAPTER NINE

PRINCIPAL NOTTINGHAM

I tried to force myself not to cry, but I felt, well...bullied, and bullied by a teacher which was even worse. The students were all laughing at me and I knew that by the time I got to my next class the word would have gotten around about my incident in first period. If newspapers worked like schools did, then we would not need the Internet to keep up with current events.

Fun Fact: Eight new islands have formed on the Earth as a result of underwater volcano eruptions since 2010.

PRINCIPAL NOTTINGHAM

It was the longest walk of my life as I went to the office. When I stepped in, there was still drying ketchup in my hair and all over my shirt. The young lady at the front desk saw me and practically screamed. She must've thought I'd fallen a few dozen times on the sidewalk and that I was covered with blood, not ketchup. I was also in tears so that hardly helped matters.

She came over to me and I heard her shouting for the school nurse. I guess I should say at this point that I am glad she did not call 911. When she got closer she realized that I was not in the middle of a medical emergency, just <u>very</u> covered with "ketchup gore."

Fun Fact: I would not want him at my school...infamous pirate Captain Blackbeard's real name was Edward Teach.

CHAPTER NINE

"Land-sakes child, what happened to you?"

"Mr. Helms got me with an exploding ketchup bottle prank." I said, defiant through my tears. "He made fun of me and I yelled at him that I knew he had done this to me for beating his team at baseball yesterday and he sent me to the Principal's office. He would not even let me clean myself first."

At this time, I was full-blown in tears and this caused some of the ketchup to drip on the floor and indeed it did look like I was dripping blood. She actually did a double-take at the sight, but then said nothing, but walked me over to a sink in the bathroom and cleaned me up as best as

Tsunami Fact: A tsunami at sea is barely noticeable, being merely a small wavelet. It is not until it reaches near shore that it becomes a large wave.

she could. She placed a reassuring hand on my shoulder and said to me "You'll be ok, promise!"

I felt like at least SOMEONE in the school was going to be nice to me and she was. "That man can be so mean at times!" She whispered this under her breath, but I think she meant for me to hear it.

She seemed almost timid about walking me to the door of Principal Nottingham. She knocked on the door and I heard a gruff "Come in." and I could understand why; Principal Nottingham was not a warm and kind man. I was escorted in and

---

Fun fact: Prinicpal Nottingham is loosely inspired by the Vice Principal at the Middle School I attended, though he was nowhere near as mean.

he pointed at a chair in front of his desk without saying anything.

His expression said it all. I remember a face I had made when I had been coerced by my uncle into trying grapefruit juice. Now imagine that face magnified one hundred times and this was the sour look Principal Nottingham gave me.

I looked at him. He was a tall, slender man with thinning black hair. Actually, the hair he had made him almost look like he was wearing a clown head because of how it formed around his scalp. However, if he were a clown, he was not

---

Arizona Fact: I lived in Mesa, Arizona myself from 1994-1999 and it was not uncommon to see people walking around openly with guns in a holster…at least at the time. I am not sure if things have changed since then.

the happy kind of one and he certainly did not make me feel like laughing.

"So, you are Mr. Finley." He said this matter-of-factly. "The new student who moved from the frontier state of Arizona; from cowboy hats and tumbleweeds, and country music to our much more temperate and educated state."

He apparently thought less of Arizona than I did. I had not been particularly fond of the weather there and there WERE a lot of cowboy hats and far too many "MAKE AMERICA GREAT" hats I agreed.

Personal Statement: I am obviously not a fan of Donald Trump.

CHAPTER NINE

That being said, I did not expect a school principal to be so blunt, and to say such things.

"This is not the wild west young man. Back in Tucson or wherever you are from, you may feel free to treat teachers with disrespect, but not here!"

Fun Fact: There are earthquakes on the moon; they are called "Moonquakes". No, I am not joking.

PRINCIPAL NOTTINGHAM

"But he...he...pranked me!" This took a lot for me to say as I swear that Nottingham's eyes glowed red as they burned into my own, almost as if he were some supernatural monster taking the form of a principal; fire breathing from his noise. It WOULD explain a lot.

"Well then, if that is your defense, maybe we should call your parents..."

I gulped, knowing the next hour or so would be quite uncomfortable.

Tsunami Fact: In the sea, a tsunami can move as fast as a jet engine, 500 mph!

CHAPTER TEN

REQUIEM FOR A STOMACH

D ad was NOT happy to hear from Principal Nottingham. For myself, I was equally unhappy to hear him deliver a very slanted, one-sided account of what had happened. In his description, I had shaken the ketchup bottle so hard that it had popped the cap off and splashed me with ketchup.

He further suggested that I had refused to clean myself so I could elicit sympathy from

---

Fun Fact: During the Civil War, spies could "tap" into telegraph lines and steal messages. Early hackers?

REQUIEM FOR A STOMACH

Mrs. Ackerstein (the lady at the front desk) by making her think I was injured and that the ketchup was blood and not ketchup.

Now my dad as I said was a consummate prankster. However, one thing he was not, was a fool. Nor was he a man who let someone slander his son. I could hear him practically scream at Principal Nottingham.

He knew the "Exploding Ketchup Bottle" prank all too well. He informed the good principal that Mr. Helms had actually directed his pitcher the day before to throw at me yesterday and that the look on his face when he lost said it all. He

Shameless Book Plug: *Rising Tide: Dark Innocence – The Maura DeLuca Trilogy – Book One* by Claudette Melanson

would NOT sit idly by while this man tried to seek his petty revenge on his son and that if he had to drive down there to pick me up, there'd be trouble in the form of an attorney.

I had assumed that when dad was done yelling that Principal Nottingham would have a response that would put both dad and me in our place. No, he was actually a bit shaken and it took him a second to regain his composure.

"Well Mr. Finley, this IS the first day of school. I strongly do not believe Mr. Helms did anything to embarrass your son, but considering that he is new to this school and this city, maybe he felt the pressure and I am prepared to

---

Fun Fact: The *Livyatan Melvillei* was a prehistoric predatory whale that could reach nearly 60 feet! It was named after Herman Melville, the author of *Moby Dick!*

forget this incident and we can move forward without further animosity. I will speak to Mr. Helms and we will smooth this over."

The bell rang to end the period. Now this school was on the "Block Schedule". This meant that on Mondays and Wednesdays, we did periods one, three, and five for about two hours each. Tuesdays and Thursdays we did periods two, four, and six. One Fridays, we did all six periods for one hour each. The bell meant that half of the students went for third period, the other half went for lunch, and would go to third

---

Fun Fact: The game series *Five Nights at Freddy's* set a record for the most game sequels release in one year. I should know, my son bought most of them.

period afterwards. I was in the group of students who went to lunch after the first bell.

"Go to lunch." Principal Nottingham said tersely. He had ended the call with my dad who had calmed down, realizing he did not want to make matters worse than they were now. I did not say anything, but went to lunch.

I gave a nod of thanks to Mrs. Ackerstein and she smiled at me. "Try to enjoy the rest of your day Hugo." I gave a grateful smile back at her.

"Thank you, I will." Famous last words of course.

Fun Fact: We had the block schedule when I was in Junior High, Middle School, and High School. Most of the students HATED getting the first lunch; it made the rest of the day drag out.

REQUIEM FOR A STOMACH

I walked out into the courtyard and saw that it was quite lively. The line to buy food had shrunk since I was arriving a little late and so there were lots of my fellow students lined up at benches eating a variety of food brought from home or purchased from the school.

There was a tap on my shoulder and as I turned around, there was Bryson along with Liam and Marcus. Each of them was holding cafeteria-purchased mozzarella sticks and tater tots; not a healthy lunch, but it looked good. I had not brought my lunch, so would need to buy mine.

Fun Fact: The last name Finley is inspired by one of my favorite all-time baseball players, Steve Finley who was an amazing outfielder for the San Diego Padres.

CHAPTER TEN

"Hurry up and grab some lunch Hugo." Bryson said. "We will save you a seat over at the benches." He pointed at an area in the corner that was unoccupied.

"Thanks, I'll be right there." I said with a smile. It was good that I had made great friends like Bryson, Liam, and Marcus. I walked quickly into the cafeteria and saw that there was a sign that said "Pizza Monday! All pizza is 50% off today!"

Fun Fact: Approximately 3 billion pizzas are sold in the United States each year. This does not include frozen pizzas.

REQUIEM FOR A STOMACH

Well, I could not pass that up, so I bought two large slices of pizza for a dollar each. It looked good, though it had that orange grease practically dripping off of it. I didn't care, I mean has anyone ever really had a BAD pizza?

As I walked away, I thought I heard the lunch lady mutter "It's your stomach kid." This was accompanied by a small chuckle. I simply shrugged and rushed to join my friends.

I reached the courtyard and well I am not sure if there really are such things as omens, but something splatted on my head. I looked at my reflection in a nearby window and saw that it was bird poop; a seagull (which my dad refers to as a "rat with wings") had dropped a bomb and

---

(Woefully UN)Fun Fact: Yes, I have had a bad pizza. There was this place I won't name, but anytime I ate there, I always ended up with an awful stomachache!

nailed my head dead-center. I probably should have noticed that the courtyard was filled with birds; seagulls, pigeons, and a few doves were pretty much everywhere.

Of course, it was only natural that a bunch of people saw it happen and not for the first time that morning did I find myself laughed at.

"Don't worry about it, come over here!" It was Marcus.

I walked over, fuming mad, but at least happy I would not be eating alone. I joined them and

---

Fun Fact: The Coelacanth was believed to have gone extinct 66 million years ago, but was "rediscovered" in 1938 off the coast of South Africa!

saw that in addition to Liam and Marcus, I was joined by two new friends. Liam explained they were Evan and Ava, a brother and sister that they had gone to elementary school with. Marcus added that "They are cool."

(LEFT TO RIGHT: EVAN, AVA, AND HUGO)

Ava took a bottle of water and poured it on a napkin and rather kindly cleaned off my head. She did it carefully so that none of it ended up on my face.

"Thanks!" I said, very gratefully. I then saw that my friends, old and new were staring at me in frightened shock.

Fun Fact: Seagulls are one of the few animals that can drink salt water. They have a special gland that eliminates excess salt from the body.

CHAPTER TEN

"What?" I asked, a bit taken aback.

"Dude, you bought the school's pizza?" Bryson asked.

"No Bryson." Evan said, correcting him. "He bought TWO pizzas!"

"No way!" Bryson said.

Liam and Marcus were patting my shoulder. "Tough break."

"Whatever are you guys talking about? Its pizza, not Brussels Sprouts!"

Fun Fact: Kids do not like Brussels Sprouts because their taste buds have not developed yet. Oh, also because they taste horrible. I never made my kids try them either.

REQUIEM FOR A STOMACH

Ava frowned at me. "Do yourself a favor, don't eat it."

I shook my head. I figured my friends were kidding me. "It's ok, I'll go ahead and eat it."

Evan had a mortified look on his face as if he thought I were about to consume a fatal poison. I laughed. It was funny, but a transparent attempt to spook me and I would not fall for it.

Now it was their turn to shake their heads. "Ok, but we warned you." Marcus said and I saw that he was restraining a laugh.

Fun Fact: The Box Jellyfish is often called the world's most venomous creature.

CHAPTER TEN

"Whatever." I said, laughing at their very obvious attempt to frighten me. "If one of you wants a slice, just ask."

The head shaking increased and for a second, I considered listening to them; but only for a second.

I ate my pizza and they let the matter drop. It was only fifteen minutes of the thirty-minute lunch we were allotted, but it seemed we got to know each other well in that short time span.

The bell for third period rang and I was happy to see that Liam, Bryson, Evan, and Ava all had Mr. Raines for English and also for History at fifth period, so we'd be in the same room and same seats together the rest of the day.

Tsunami Fact: Often it is not the first wave that is the biggest. Many times, the third or fourth is the worst.

REQUIEM FOR A STOMACH

Of course, in looking back, it would be hard to say who would regret my lunch choices more just a few minutes after the class started.

BWA-HA-HA-HA-HA-HA!!!!!

Fun Facts: The tiny cookie cutter shark has been known to attack submarines!

CHAPTER ELEVEN

A FOUL WIND BLOWS

N ow THAT was a loud bell. When it rang, I swear I saw the windows shake! There was no question that it was time for third period to begin. I was calmer now, the events of first period and my confrontations with both Mr. Helms and Principal Nottingham nearly forgotten.

(POSTER FOR THE NOVEL *LORD OF THE WOLVES* BY JAMES MATLACK RANEY ABOVE)

I had five new friends and this would make this school year bearable, even if Mr. Helms was

---

Fun Fact: In *E. T. The Extra Terrestrial* (1982), famous actor Harrison Ford makes a cameo, but the scene was deleted from the final cut of the film.

A FOUL WIND BLOWS

determined to treat me badly. Besides, I had a plan to get revenge upon him, but more on that later.

Mr. Raines arrived at the classroom. He was a tall man which short-cropped gray hair and thick, square glasses to accompany his rather serious expression. As he leaned over to put his briefcase down, I saw a small bald spot in the middle of his head and there was a small giggle from some of my classmates, but he either did not hear them or just did not care.

"Hello ladies and gentlemen. I am Dr. Fred Raines and from what I see, about half of you

---

Fun Fact: At my school and in high school, the principal seemed hardly more than a figurehead, the Vice Principals were the ones that the students were afraid of.

will be sitting here with me for the better part of four hours." He remained silent, perhaps waiting to see if he heard any groans, but was instead greeted by an equal silence to that of the size of the classroom. He seemed unmoved by this and continued.

"My job here is to teach you literature and for many of you, history. Now, I cannot promise you this class will be fun. I am not here for you to be entertained."

This did garner a reaction, one of frowns and other disappointed looks. NO ONE liked a stern and strict teacher. Then Dr. Raines smiled.

"Now, with that out of the way, I am of the opinion that students will learn more if I make

---

Fun Fact: The 1898 book *The Wreck of the Titan* by Morgan Robertson eerily presaged the Titanic disaster.

A FoUL WiND BLoWS

it enjoyable, so again, while I can promise nothing, I will do my best to make learning the subjects at least bearable. If you will give me the respect of your undivided attention, I'll give you the same consideration as I present the course and try and make these hours pass painlessly. Deal?"

The response was nearly unilateral; a chorus of head nods and voices saying "yes".

"Good then I'll begin. Let's speak briefly about our curriculum for the semester."

I could tell that Dr. Raines was going to be a good teacher to have. I enjoy reading and

---

Fun Fact: The first ever video game is believed to be *Tennis for Two*. It was invented in 1958 by Physicist William Higinbotham.

history has always been exciting. I'm sure many do not agree with me, but think of it how my dad describes it; a long journal where you get to read about other people's foul-ups. He used to tell me "Yeah, I'm cynical, but if George Washington can mess up and still be a hero, well there is hope for the rest of us."

Dr. Raines shared we would be reading *Tom Sawyer* and *Huckleberry Finn*, two books I had already read and enjoyed. I began to smile in anticipation, but then something happened to make it go away.

Literary Comment: *Tom Sawyer* and *Huckleberry Finn* are fun adventure stories, equally humorous and exciting. Give them a read; you will not regret it!

A FOUL WIND BLOWS

My stomach was seized by a sharp pain and it began to feel like my belly was being tapped from the inside by a few dozen fingers. I was very uncomfortable and I began to sweat. Ava looked over at me and whispered "Oh no, the pizza has struck Hugo in English class."

Liam, Bryson, and Evan also gave me concerned looks. One of them, I don't know who, whispered "Start the countdown, he's going to blow."

Sure enough, I tried to hold it in, but I failed on an epic level. Now there is no shame in

---

Fun Fact: Mark Twain, the author of *The Adventures of Tom Sawyer* and *Huckleberry Finn* was born Samuel Langhorne Clemens. Mark Twain was his pen name.

farting; I mean it happens. However, in school, surrounded by a class of eleven and twelve-year-olds, it is probably the most mortifying thing ever.

Moreover, it got worse. Not only was it loud, it was long; long enough to catch the attention of the whole classroom, including Dr. Raines. Oh, by the way, it smelled at least five times as bad as the beef jerky ones in the car I had bombed my dad with.

To add fuel to the fire, I did not stop at one. As a matter of fact, after five of them, each of them loud enough to be heard over the laughter

---

Sad Fact: Unfortunately, this event happened to a fellow classmate of mine. I have no idea what he ate, but he was ridiculed for a couple of weeks over this.

A FoUL WiND BLoWS

of the classroom, I stopped counting. I heard a resounding chorus of "Better check his pants!"

"Everyone be quiet!" Dr. Raines shouted, his pleasant demeanor replaced by a stern countenance. He walked over to me and said "Come on outside Hugo." His voice was commanding, but it did not sound angry, instead he almost sounded sympathetic. I followed him outside.

He walked me around the corner, outside of the prying eyes and ears of my classmates. He looked at me and I looked back, struggling and barely succeeding in holding another burst of gas in. I was pretty sure he was trying to

---

Fun Fact: Some beetles fart to attract mates. It never worked for me when I tried it. Just kidding.

determine if this act of mine was intentional or not.

"Mr. Finley, did you eat the school's pizza at lunch?"

I thought I was going to throw up now. I mean this day had been a roller coaster ride, and not a fun one. However, I managed to stammer out "Yes, sir."

"Well, you did not know better, but those pizzas are rather greasy and potent. That slice can be enough to upset anyone's stomach."

Fun Fact: Termites fart more than any animal on Earth!

A FOUL WIND BLOWS

"Uh, I had two." I said timidly and my face was red, although whether that was due to how sick I felt or embarrassment was anyone's guess.

Dr. Raines looked at me as if I had just swallowed poison...and perhaps I had. "My word Hugo, NO ONE ever eats two of those things! Well, I think you know where you have to go."

He pointed down the hallway and there was no mistaking where he was sending me.

I turned away as I failed to fight back tears.

Fun Fact(?): I am not sure if this is true, but I read that farts have been clocked at speeds of ten feet per second; who in the world decided to measure that?

CHAPTER ELEVEN

I then answered "Yes sir." So off I went back to Principal Nottingham's office.

Tsunami Fact: An earthquake-triggered rockslide in Alaska caused a tsunami in Lituya Bay. The waves reached over 1,700 feet in height!

CHAPTER TWELVE

NOTTINGHAM AGAIN!

Chances are, no one gets sent to the Principal twice in one day. I would say the odds are better for snow to fall in the summer than for any kid in school seeing Principal Nottingham twice in one year as a matter of fact. Who'd want to see this monster even once in a lifetime?

Yet, here I was, sweat dripping off of my forehead and walking down the lonely corridors

---

Tsunami Fact: In 1645 BCE, a volcanic eruption generated a tsunami that devastated the island of Crete.

towards the main office. My stomach had ceased protesting my earlier lunch and I was feeling better, but the damage had been done. Oddly, I had the strange feeling that the gas I had released in the class would follow me for a long time, like a puppy; a really smelly puppy.

MY PET FART ANDREA

As I walked by an empty classroom, I took a second to see my reflection in a window and boy did I look bad. I had a shirt still covered with ketchup, my face, while clean, looked pale and I think I had a few wrinkles, or was that a trick of the sunlight reflecting on the glass? I tried to smile, but my lips would not obey me. Instead of smiling, my lips were quivering and my eyes

Fun Fact: The Messerschmitt Me-163 *Komet* was a rocket-powered fighter aircraft. It could only fly for seven-and-a-half minutes before it needed to land.

were watering up, preparing to unleash a torrent of tears.

Remember that quiet voice in my head I mentioned earlier? You know, the one that tells you that danger is near? The closer I got to the main office, the louder it shouted, but I was even more terrified of not going to the office, so I was going there. Still, the worst part was that I was going to need to explain to the Principal why I was there this time; he was not going to be forewarned by Dr. Raines, or so I assumed.

The hallways seemed to stretch out forever and I imagined myself as a bold adventurer,

---

Old joke: Three men walk into a bar; you'd think the 2nd and 3rd guy would've walked around it. Ha ha ha!

surrounded by dragons, orcs, and goblins, braving the dangers of an evil wizard's castle, and that evil wizard was Principal Nottingham.

If only that were the real threat, which was far less frightening than facing a year of detention or whatever awful punishment surely awaited me; a fate that I doubted even my dad could not rescue me from this time.

Mrs. Ackerstein's face when she saw me was a mixture of horror and surprise. I must have looked ghastly to her with my saddened face and I thought again she was on the verge of calling 911. Of course, her surprise was any

---

Fun Fact: The Tyrannosaurus Rex could sprint up to 20 miles per hour!

CHAPTER TWELVE

student in the school daring to venture into the lair of the dragon (that being Principal Nottingham) again.

"Hugo, my dear boy, why are you here?"

"Dr. Raines sent me here. I did something bad, but I didn't mean to."

"I'm sure you didn't dear." She gave a hesitant look at his office. "I guess you better go in there."

Fun Fact: Feed a cow onions and do you know what their milk will taste like? Answer: Onions.

NOTTINGHAM AGAIN!

I slowly walked towards his door and I actually imagined him as a dragon of sorts, ready to breathe fire at me; a fire which would consume and burn me for the rest of the school year. I gave his door a gentle knock.

A PLUG FOR THE NOVEL RISING TIDE BY CLAUDETTE MELANSON

"Who's there?" he said tersely.

"Hu...Hu...Hugo Finley." I said.

"Again? What did you do this time?" He sounded exasperated, but there was also anticipation in his tone, as if he were happy for a chance to have at me again. "Come in!"

Fun Fact: Polar Bears are excellent swimmers and have been found many miles from land.

CHAPTER TWELVE

I stepped in and did not wait for him to gesture towards his chair again. I walked over and sat down. My hands were sweaty and the inside of my mouth tasted like I had swallowed my socks. I felt sick from my head to my toe and as I looked up at him, I could see he was thoroughly enjoying my displeasure. He looked a lot like some kind of troll with a horrible unibrow and uneven glasses and it creeped me out.

PRINCIPAL NOTTINGHAM -- A TROLL WITH A UNIBROW

"So, Hugo, please tell me, why are you here?"

I blurted out the truth, or I began to. "I farted a bunch of times in class." That was true,

---

Fun Fact: It takes the planet Neptune 164.8 Earth years to orbit the sun.

but it did not exactly put the events in the best light. It made me sound like I had done so out of an impish sense of mischief; something a troublemaker or juvenile delinquent would do.

The edges of his forehead seemed to stretch out and for a moment, I swear he grew a third eyebrow as he stared at me. "I can see that you are going to be a special case Mr. Finley. Maybe one hour of detention for every act of nastiness you inflicted on Dr. Raines and your classmates; yes, would that teach you some level of decorum?"

The phone rang in his office. Principal Nottingham answered it. "Yeah? Yes Dr. Raines,

---

Fun Fact: The Bull Shark can live in fresh water and salt water. Scary thought huh?

he is here. He just confessed the whole thing to me. What? No, Dr. Raines, I doubt it. He seemed pretty guilty to me. You what? All right." He sighed, a look of frustration etched on his face. "Here, take the phone."

"Uh...hello?" I said, not knowing what was going on.

"Hugo, why on Earth did you go to the Principal's office?"

"Because you told me to. I am in trouble for what happened."

Fun Fact: The 1998 *Godzilla* movie was so unpopular, that many fans refer to it as "G.I.N.O." which stands for "Godzilla In Name Only". I agree, it was an awful flick!

NOTTiNGHAM AGAiN!

"Are you joking? Hugo, I am not a monster, I certainly would not send you to the Principal because you suffered a stomach upset! Cripes son, I meant for you to go to the nurse! Now get there and take a nap until the end of the period and I'll see you after the bell rings."

"Ok, uh...th...th...thank you."

Dr. Raines hung up. I looked at Principal Nottingham and he looked about as disappointed as any man I had ever seen. He really had his heart set on giving me detention. Instead I was being told I could rest and relax. "Get to the nurse's office, but I do not want to see you in here again today!"

Spoiler Alert: Principal Nottingham WILL see Hugo again today, read on.

CHAPTER TWELVE

I wiped a shower of sweat from my forehead and gratefully left his office, but left a silent cloud of stench for him as a present for him to enjoy.

Fun Fact: Since Hugo is sweating above…did you know that humans have between 2-4 million sweat glands spread across their body?

CHAPTER THIRTEEN
OH NO! NOT AGAIN!

Nurse Sarvis was a young woman fresh out of nursing school. Her mother had been the school nurse for many years and had retired and whether coincidence or not, they had passed the job onto her daughter. I was embarrassed to tell such a beautiful woman what had happened, but I did and she did not laugh or crack a smile or otherwise indicate she thought my misfortune was funny. She DID however tell me never to eat the school's pizza; and if I did, never exceed one slice.

She gave me a lemon-lime soda and told me to drink it. I had never drunk a soda before, my dad had warned me it could rot out my teeth.

Fun Fact: Soda was originally used for medical reasons. Carbonation was added to it later.

OH NO! NOT AGAIN!

However, I drank it and a few minutes later, endured still another embarrassing moment when I burped loud enough that I am surprised the windows did not shake! Fortunately, she did not even look in my direction.

She had me lay down and my head had barely hit the pillow before I was fast asleep. I guess this day had really taken a lot out of me. While I was out, I had more than a few dreams about

---

Fun Fact: The "burp" above is a tribute or homage to the comic strip *Calvin and Hobbes,* my all-time favorite.

my day thus far and it was during this brief interlude in my day that I came up with the perfect revenge for Mr. Helms.

Nurse Sarvis woke me and surprised me with a t-shirt that I could wear in place of my ruined one. "It's a little large, but it is clean." I thanked her and she walked me to the door saying "Come back if you begin feeling sick again."

The bell rang right after and somewhat nervously I began walking towards Dr. Raines' class, this time for United States History. I dreaded the looks I would get from the classmates that had witnessed the event and

---

Fun Fact: If you are reading this page, you've just been "Rick-Rolled". Look up the term online ☺

the ones that would be arriving and had surely heard about my rather epically bad day thus far.

I heard a voice say "Hugo!" and I turned to see it was Bryson, walking with Ava and Evan. I dreaded this as even friends could be rather cruel when someone did the thing I did. I cannot say I would blame them; after all, they smelled the worst of it.

I said nothing, my face saying it all. I was embarrassed and ashamed.

Bryson put his hand on my shoulder. "Hey, don't worry about it. All you did was warn us never to eat two slices."

Fun Fact: The whale shark is the largest fish (and shark) in the ocean. However, it is harmless and is known as a "gentle giant". Divers often enjoy swimming with them.

CHAPTER THIRTEEN

"It could've happened to any of us!" Bryson said and he clapped me on the back. I felt better and I smiled back at them. Maybe The incident would not be soon forgotten, but my friends would not be teasing me.

I reached Dr. Raines class and he stopped me. He had a somewhat mischievous smile on his face, but it was not a mean one. He asked me "Are you all right son?"

"Yes sir." I said, still embarrassed.

"Good to hear it. Now don't ever eat two of the school pizzas again."

Fun Fact: The Basenji breed of dog does not generally bark. They yodel or chortle a lot; they can be quite loud.

OH NO! NOT AGAIN!

"You got that right sir."

"Go on then and sit down."

The bell rang as I took my seat. Dr. Raines conducted the class as if nothing had happened. The bell rang and we exited the classroom. It was then that I saw another student walk behind Bryson and began flicking his ear. Bryson was not liking it, but the kid behind him was much larger and it was clear he was just going to have to deal with it.

Fun Fact: The Tuatara is the oldest living reptile, dating back 200 million years. It can live up to 100 years itself. Despite its appearance, it is not actually a lizard.

CHAPTER THIRTEEN

Well, this would not do. "Hey, leave him alone, he did not do anything to you." I whispered at him. I saw on his folder the name "James Lowes".

"You gonna stop me?" he said and his ace was threatening.

"Flick his ear again and you'll find out."

He scowled at me, but did not do anything further. However, after the class bell rang, which indicated our long school day was over, he was again bothering Bryson. I stepped in front of him. "Leave him alone!"

Fun Fact: The first Dr. Pepper bottle sold over 130 years ago, in 1885!

OH NO! NOT AGAIN!

It was then I saw that James was a good two or three inches and forty or more pounds heavier than me. I decided I was not going to back down. I stood firm and gave him a threatening look. "I'll make you eat the sidewalk if you touch him again."

"What did you say? Say again what you will do to me, I couldn't hear you."

"I'll make you eat the sidewalk!"

"Will you now?" The voice came from behind me. I turned around and sure enough, it was Principal Nottingham.

Needless to say, I ended up in his office again.

Fun Fact: The Maine Coon is the largest domesticated cat in the world, reaching as long as four feet in length!

CHAPTER FOURTEEN
A NIGHT OF PLOTTING

Principal Nottingham seemed to take great pleasure in calling my dad. I was frantic, again nearing tears. I wondered how this creep got to be a principal of a school when he was so mean. He did not listen to me as I protested that James was picking on Bryson. Bryson had been told to "stay out of it" when he also tried to point out James as a bully.

Fun Fact: Probably no surprise, but I based Principal Nottingham after the wicked Sheriff of Nottingham from the story of *Robin Hood*.

A NIGHT OF PLOTTING

At least James could do nothing further. Dr. Raines had stepped outside and he was not about to do something in the presence of a teacher. Ava and Evan had also witnessed it, but had been told to "butt out!" rather crudely, again by Principal Nottingham.

WHO SAYS SEAGULLS CAN'T BE HEROES?

He smiled at me, a really wicked smile. "Your father will be right over and he does not sound happy." He cracked his knuckles and I made a face at him, grossed out by the noise.

Fun Fact: The Magic 8-Ball has twenty possible answers; one-half of them are positive.

"Maybe you'd care to mitigate your punishment by confessing that you were picking a fight and acting like a juvenile delinquent? Surely your good fortune can't last forever; I will eventually have you in detention anyways; so, I frankly think that you might as well learn your lesson now."

Good fortune? He called this day good fortune? I could not imagine how this day could go worse, but then remembered that my dad was on his way and it was about to go from bad to horrible! It did not help that at that moment he resembled Frankenstein's Monster.

Fun Fact: Godfrey Auty, a British test pilot earned the title "Most Likely to Eject" when he was scheduled to test the experimental Bristol 188 jet. The jet itself was derisively nicknamed "The Flaming Pencil."

A NiGHT oF PLoTTiNG

I kept my mouth shut, which was the last thing Nottingham expected (or wanted). He was frankly hoping I would argue with him or yell, but I knew enough to keep my lip zipped. I just sat there with my hands in my lap and stared downward, waiting for my dad to show up and to endure his wrath.

Mrs. Ackerstein walked in after what seemed like an eternity. "Mr. Finley's father is here." She said it almost fearfully.

Nottingham smiled. "Please show him in." He stood up as my dad walked in.

Dad looked at me. "Hugo, please wait in the hall."

Fun Fact: Ok, maybe not so fun. The F2A *Brewster Buffalo* fighter used in WWII is widely considered one of the worst fighter planes ever used by the United States.

CHAPTER FOURTEEN

I stepped outside and saw that Liam, Marcus, Bryson, Ava, and Evan were sitting there, their eyes filled with concern. I had expected my dad to yell at me and boy did he ever yell...at Principal Nottingham!

"You have some nerve! My son was assaulted by his first period teacher with a revenge prank and you blame him? Then he had a medical problem and you again accuse him of mischief? Then he sticks up for his friend and you automatically choose my son as the scapegoat instead of the bully who started it?"

Fun Fact: Shock Rock musician Alice Cooper claims to have come up with his stage name using a *Ouija* board.

A Night of Plotting

I could see shadows under the door and if I was not mistaking, my dad, who was normally not confrontational was sticking his finger in Nottingham's face. "I'm putting you on notice! If you EVER mistreat my son, if you ever give him biased treatment or make another inappropriate remark about his home state, I'll see you in court!"

He opened the door and strode out and if this were a cartoon, there'd be smoke coming from his ears. He then closed the door and began walking towards the exit, but not before turning around and shouting "n00b!"

Fun Fact: The XF-85 Goblin jet was classified as a "parasite Fighter", designed to take off from a larger aircraft. As you may have guessed, it was a complete failure.

CHAPTER FOURTEEN

I was not sure he really got the meaning, but then again, Nottingham would be the king of all n00bs, so maybe he did. Anyways, dad then turned to me. "Come on Hugo, let's get out of here!" He looked at my friends "Thanks kids, you guys need to head home too."

With that, he gently took my backpack and headed towards the door, me following him.

"Have a nice day Mr. Finley!" Mrs. Ackerstein said and I could swear she was restraining a smile at my dad's outburst.

The ride home was quiet. After leaving, dad had calmed down and it was clear he did not to

---

Fun Fact: I use primarily a drawing style that is designed to resemble computer games – thus this pic has an Easter Egg somewhere. It should be easy to find.

say anything until he was relaxed. On the way to the car, he had asked me if I was ok and with my answer that I was, had fallen into his current state of silence.

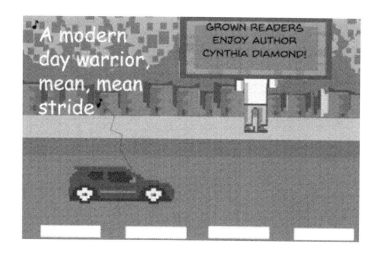

We arrived home and mom was reclining on the couch. I could tell she was again not feeling well and once more dad told me not to worry. I had grown a bit annoyed at this and wanted to shout at them "Hey! If you want me to act like a grownup, then talk to me like one." However, I'd endured enough drama today and did not think I

Fun Fact: George Washington is often called the father of our country in the United States. Another George Washington is the father of instant coffee; he invented it in 1910.

could stomach any more stress; it would wait until tomorrow.

I decided instead that I had to plan for the next few days. James Lowes was on my mind.

Actually, so was Mr. Helms. I had not been raised to seek revenge, but I also had a lot of my dad in me. I therefore had a few rather interesting pranks in mind. Of course, my next class with Mr. Helms was not until Wednesday since this school operated on the block schedule. I also was uncertain about my next class with James, so would have a bit of time to consider my plots. I came down for dinner and mom was feeling better again. Her and I

Fun Fact: The first video game to use synthesized speech was *Stratovox* known in Japan as *Speak & Rescue* (1980).

A NiGHT oF PLoTTiNG

enjoyed a nice dinner together while dad did some paperwork. Mom listened as I spoke about my first day of school. My mood and tone was upbeat, but in my mind, I contemplated balancing the scales and promised myself I'd stay out of trouble on Tuesday. Of course, one should never make a promise that they cannot keep, as the next day taught me all too well.

Fun Fact: In the movie *Tron* (1982), there is a "Hidden Mickey" in the movie as the Solar Sail flies over the digital landscape.

PART III

TUESDAY: THE HITS 🏐 JUST 👊 KEEP ON COMING!

CHAPTER FIFTEEN

LADY PAIN

awoke the next morning and mom still seemed her old self, so I assumed that whatever had laid her out was just some kind of bug. I enjoyed pancakes and sausage for breakfast instead of my preferred one and then grabbed my backpack and allowed dad to take me to school.

I had never been a Boy Scout, but their motto of "Be prepared" is a good one, so unbeknownst to dad and mom, I packed a few things in my

---

Fun Fact: The Boy Scouts date back to the early 1900s.

backpack just in case anything like Monday decided to rear its ugly head.

I arrived at school and Liam and Marcus were entering the grounds with Ava and Evan.

"How'd it go yesterday with your dad?" Ava asked.

"It went fine, he knew I had not done anything wrong. He did not say much afterwards. I think he knew I did not want to talk about it and respected my privacy."

"Hey", said Evan. "I heard you have Journalism for second period.

Tsunami Fact: The states in the U.S. at greatest risk for tsunamis are Hawaii, Alaska, Washington, Oregon, and California.

CHAPTER FIFTEEN

I nodded. "Yeah, I love writing, I thought I'd do a column on pranks if she will let me."

"Well, don't count on it, not with the infamous Lady Pain as your teacher." Marcus said, smiling mischievously.

"Lady Pain?" I asked, feeling a shiver course throughout my body and settling in my spine. "Why do they call her that?"

Marcus shrugged. "No one knows, but they gotta call her that for a reason right?" He smiled again at me. "So be careful." He laughed and I allowed him his private joke.

Fun Fact: Lady Pain is based loosely on a friend of mine named Suelean (pronounced "Sue Lynn") and she is just as nice as Lady Pain is in this book.

LADY PAIN

There was not much else for me to do. Ava had elected to do Journalism, so she went with me and when I got there, Bryson was in the class also. There were a pair of empty seats next to him, so the two of us joined him. He smiled at us and I saw that he was already scanning the material on the laptop that each of us had on our desks about performing interviews and properly obtaining quotes.

The bell rang and I felt a lump well up in my throat. Many of the students also looked up, expectantly nervous. The door opened as the

---

Fun Fact: I wrote for the school newspaper in high school, the paper was called *The Arrow* and still is.

bell rang and in she stepped. She walked over to the chalkboard and she turned around and for the first time, I beheld her; the infamous...Lady Pain.

I then smiled. She was a little over five feet tall and while it was clear she had hit the gym frequently, she had an easy smile and was hardly imposing at all. Marcus had to have been pulling my leg, there was no way this teacher could be mean and as fearful as he had suggested.

"Greetings class. My name is Sue Simpson and together we will be putting out the *Harkin*

Classic Game Moment: In the computer basketball game *One on One: Julius Erving and Larry Bird* (1983), your player can break the backboard and a janitor will come out and yell at you...HILARIOUS!

Herald. I would like to leap right in and have all of you submit your idea for an article for the next month's edition."

The class overall went well. I wrote my idea, working quietly and spent nearly the entire two-hour period writing out a potential article on "Fun, but harmless pranks".

I frankly did not think she would accept it. However, when she called for us to hand in our work, I gave her mine and she smiled. "It has possibilities...we'll see what we can do with this."

Tsunami Fact: In 2004, the Indian Ocean tsunami was caused by an earthquake with the energy of 23,000 atomic bombs!

CHAPTER FIFTEEN

I gazed up at her in surprise, but then the bell rang and she said "Class dismissed" and turned away and walked over to her desk. It was now time for lunch, and like yesterday's, it would be one I would not soon forget.

Classic Game Fact: The computer game *Maniac Mansion* (1987) has seven main characters, you can accomplish multiple different endings in it; not bad for a 30 year old game!

CHAPTER SIXTEEN

ELIMINATION GAME

Ava, Bryson, and I headed off to lunch and it was a sure thing that I would not eat the pizza today, nor probably ever. Actually, as I placed my books into my backpack, I noticed that mom had packed a small freezer pack along with a salami-and-(extra-sharp) cheese sandwich.

I saw as we were walking that there was a game of Four Square going on and I am a big fan

---

Fun Fact: The Commodore 64, one of the greatest computers of its day, known for amazing games, had less computing power than a modern calculator!

of that game. I also am about one or two inches taller than most of the players my age, so could match up favorably even against the seventh and eighth-graders. I began munching down on my sandwich and as soon as I finished, I ran over. Bryson and Ava both smiled at me and Bryson yelled "We'll join you in a few minutes!"

The line was only about six or seven people, so I figured I would be playing soon and planned to dominate the square until the bell rang for me to get to my next class.

I was three people away when one of the students, a boy my age who I knew as Mike

---

Classic Video Game Fact: Ok, not a classic, but the "E. T." Game cartridge for Atari was so bad, they buried unsold copies in a landfill!

CHAPTER SIXTEEN

Ripley pushed me out of the way. "Thanks for holding my place nerd."

I nudged him back. "Your place is at the back of the line! No taking cuts!"

He had a few friends with him and they surrounded me, but Sandy, the lunch monitor was nearby and so they backed off. While this was going on, a few players were eliminated and I got my turn.

The ball was served to me. Now I have a unique way of playing Four Square. I have always felt that the new player in the box should

---

Classic Game Fact: The highest score that can be achieved in Pac-Man is 3,333,360 points.

not go on offense, but should play more of a defensive role. If I try to immediately knock someone out, I become the jerk of the group. So, with that, I served it gently to the person to my right. However, I did it with enough of an angle that he could not spike it back at me.

The ball moved around a bit and came back to me. Now that I had played defense once, in my opinion, it was ok to eliminate another player, so I did. I spiked the ball on the server and he was out. He calmly walked away and took his spot at the back of the line.

I saw that Mike Ripley had bullied his way to the front. He stepped into the square and

---

Classic Video Game Fact: The popularity of the Nintendo Game Mario Brothers (1983) led to a huge increase of children being named Mario. Poor Luigi, the guy gets no respect, does he?

regarded me angrily. The ball was served to me and it could not have been set up better. It bounced high, near my eyes and using both hands and all my strength, I spiked the ball on Mike's square and sent it a good ten or more feet past him; he could not return it if he had super powers.

I did not look smug, simply satisfied about putting him in his place. There was a smattering of applause. If I'd had to guess, I would have assumed that Mike Ripley was not particularly popular; bullies never truly are. I thought my elimination of him would be the end of it.

Fun Fact: I really did spike the ball on the bully that day, and yes, it went so far, he'd have needed a car to catch it.

ELiMiNATioN GAME

However, apparently he thought my place was on the ground. He turned to walk away, but then spun and hit me with a total sucker punch in the mouth, knocking me to the ground and giving me a bloody lip.

I have never considered myself a crybaby, but the events of the past two days were overwhelming and the punch hurt. Sandy came over and asked what happened and Mike and his four friends, one of them being James Lowes all said I threw the first punch. Mike grabbed his arm as if in pain to show it. I of course had done nothing wrong and the other people there knew it, but they were afraid to speak up.

Did he like carrots?: Sonic the Hedgehog was originally planned as a rabbit.

CHAPTER SIXTEEN

Sandy helped me up and gave me a really dirty look and said "You and your Arizona attitude got you what you deserve. You hit someone for no reason because he would not let you cut in front of him. I'm taking you to Principal Nottingham."

I wept as I explained my side, but she said "I do not believe you for a minute."

As angry as I was, this would have been a good time to keep my mouth shut...but I didn't.

"Nice outfit, I was wondering where my grandmother's shower curtains went." Needless to say, I was sent to Principal Nottingham again.

(Un)Fun Fact: The events above really happened to me. I am friends now with the person who punched me, but the lunch monitor was a disgrace to the school and I have never forgotten that she blamed me for getting punched.

CHAPTER SEVENTEEN

RESPONDING IN KIND

Principal Nottingham was happy to see me, especially with my bloody lip. However, he was not there to punish me. Bryson, Liam, Marcus, Evan, and Ava had ran over and pleaded my case for me. Marcus and Liam said they had known Mike Ripley since elementary school and that he had a record as a bully, including numerous in-school suspensions. He had surprisingly obliged them and called that school and it had been confirmed.

Instead, he told me to be careful what I say, since the next time, it WOULD be me in trouble.

(Modern) Classic Game Fact: The computer and console game *Minecraft* was originally called "Cave Game".

RESPONDING IN KIND

Mike Ripley would endure two weeks of after-school detention for this "first offense" and he gave me an accusing look, as if this were my fault or a plot to cause trouble and said "I hope you are happy."

I was about as defiant as I had ever been. I showed him my swollen lip and the blood on my collar and said "Do I actually LOOK happy?" and then I stormed out. I was prepared to call my dad and give him another round with the Principal if he said anything, but fortunately (or unfortunately), he said nothing and I headed for fourth period, which was Pre-Algebra.

I was both surprised and glad to see that my five friends were all headed to Shawn Lawhead's

---

Fun Fact: Giraffes are the tallest mammals on Earth and can run at speeds of up to 35 miles per hour!

class. Marcus shared that he had him for "Basic Math Principals" last year (what many people described as a "cop-out" class) and that he was a cool teacher with a fun sense of humor.

My own sense of humor (and payback) kicked into gear when I saw that Mike Ripley was in the class with me. He gave me a wicked smile and punched his fists together. He did it a few times to make his point clear.

Now my dad had made me take lessons in Aikido and Judo growing up, plus he also had me join him at the gym, so I was far from afraid. Add to that I had the ex-Marine uncle (we all

---

Fun Fact: I actually did have a teacher with the last name of Lawhead, but he taught Spanish, not Math.

seem to have one), who taught me a few dirty tricks, so I was sort of hoping he'd try again; I would NOT be caught with my guard down again.

However, I did not plan to use violence; after all what did that EVER solve? Instead I reached into my bag of tricks and smiled back at him, giving him a "Give me your best shot" look. I then pulled out what I knew would be the payback tool of all time.

Before leaving Arizona, my dad had needed to call an exterminator to deal with some mice that would not leave us alone. He had resorted to placing glue traps around the house. My dad decided that those were inhumane and chose to

---

Fun Fact: The longest recorded game of *Monopoly* lasted 70 days!

use bait traps so that he could catch them and release them away from home.

The upshot of this was that we had kept the dozen boxes of glue traps and I had decided to bring one to school. My mom always said "Fortune favors the brave and resourceful." Well, this was not brave, but by my own estimation, this plan was resourceful; or at least clever.

Mike got up to sharpen his pencil. As he did, I walked over and deftly laid a pair of them on his chair; one of them facing up, the other on

---

Another Monopoly Fact: Marvin Gardens doesn't exist. Marven Gardens is real, but there's a typo on the board that never got fixed.

top of it in a perpendicular direction facing down so it looked like a "Cross of glue traps".

I casually snuck back to my chair and reclined to watch the event unfold. I had not credited Mike with much intelligence (bullies as a whole are generally cowardly and stupid), however, he was perceptive I suppose. I know this because he sat down and quickly realized that he was stuck. Wow, this school had another Einstein.

"Stuck! I'm stuck!" He stood up and the chair lifted off of the floor with him as he looked like a hunchback now. Now like I said, I am not a

---

Another Board Game Fact: The board game *Clue* spawned a movie. It had multiple endings and which theater you went to determined which you saw. The DVD has all three of them.

crier and when I cried, it was because I was a bit overwhelmed and in pain. Mike however, cried more than I did during a whole year of being a newborn baby.

I felt sorry...for Mr. Lawhead. He had to regain control of a classroom that was laughing loudly and resisting his requests for silence. He called the school custodian, but well...in case you have never seen a glue trap, they do NOT let go. He finally had to take a pair of scissors and cut off that part of his pants, so that there was a large swath cut in them, so that his polka-dot underpants were showing.

Fun Fact: America's first steam locomotive lost a race to a horse!

RESPONDiNG iN KiND

The custodian at least had foresight. He had brought a pair of small coveralls and Mike had to put them on so that he would not be laughed at...as much. Then after he left, Mr. Lawhead finally managed to restore order.

Then of course came the moment I knew was coming, the true aftermath of my action; Principal Nottingham arrived at the classroom. Of course, NO ONE saw what I had done (actually I know my friends had witnessed it, but they remained mute on the subject).

Fun Fact: Submarines are older than you think. The first submarine was invented in 1620!

Therefore, there were no repercussions...for me. Mike Ripley was called "Sergeant Underpants" behind his back for the rest of the school year.

A closing comment on this incident; Principal Nottingham knew I had done it, but had apparently surrendered here. As he walked off, he told Mr. Lawhead "If he ever gets caught robbing a bank, just let him go; the conviction will never stick."

Fun Fact(?): It is believed that there is a Black Hole in our galaxy.

CHAPTER EIGHTEEN

FURTHER ACTS OF WAR

I had not planned for an extended campaign of payback against the bullies that had thus far made my first two days unpleasant. However, fate had other plans. I went to my Physical Education class and shared my epic exploits with Bryson and Ava, both of whom had many of the same classes as I did.

The two of us entered the gymnasium where the "Harkin Howlers" played intramural

---

Fun Fact: Sonic the Hedgehog was originally conceived as a rabbit.

FURTHER ACTS OF WAR

basketball against the other Middle Schools in the area. It was here where we would choose our course of study. The choices were soccer, aerobics, basketball, and dodgeball.

There were about twenty other students who went over to the bleachers for dodgeball. This would be a six-week series of instruction and games and then we would migrate to another course. In a nutshell, there was no avoiding aerobics. Not that I had anything against it, but it just did not sound like it would be as much fun.

As we sat there, a putrid smell filled the area. No, it was not me, but everyone looked around

---

(Un)fun Fact: Dolphins can be affected by air pollution.

to see if someone looked guilty. However, I saw that I was surrounded by twenty convincing poker faces, so apparently no one had done it. I also saw that James Lowes, the bully whom I had encountered yesterday was in our group.

He walked over to Ava and handed her a sign and said "I dare you to read this out-loud."

Now Ava and her brother are very intelligent, but we all have those moments that we wished we could take back and for Ava, this would turn out to be one of them. She read it aloud. "Eye Yam Doug Earl Hoof Hearted".

She read it loudly and it was immediately afterwards that she realized that what she

---

Fun Fact: "Bill the Pony" in the movie *The Fellowship of the Ring* was actually two men in a costume.

read sounded like she said "I am the girl who farted".

It was a given that the entire group would laugh at her. Bryson and I did not laugh, but got very mad. Bryson simmered and I could see he wanted to knock James' block off, but I whispered "Easy, I got this."

There was a cartoon that my dad said he watched as a kid called "Felix the Cat". He had a magical bag of tricks that he used to defeat bad guys and accomplish goals. Today, my backpack would fulfill that same role.

Shameless Book Plug: The *Task Force: Gaea* series by David Berger.

CHAPTER EIGHTEEN

I had a chocolate bar in my backpack. I had made what some would think was the unfortunate decision not to keep it near the ice pack. In this case though, luck (or perhaps karma) was on my side. The bar had melted, yet the chocolate did not stick too bad to the wrapper. With ninja-like precision, I placed the melted bar on his seat. I then made myself scarce and went to the bathroom and hoped that its design was like that of my last school.

I was in luck. The door had a small coat hook extending from it and on the floor was a small, rubber trash can. It had been completely emptied and so was light. I slowly picked it up, turned it upside down, and hung it precariously

---

Fun Fact: Lightning is roughly five times hotter than the surface of the sun!

from the hook, and then gently closed the door. I then dashed back into the gym, just in time to see James sit down on the candy bar.

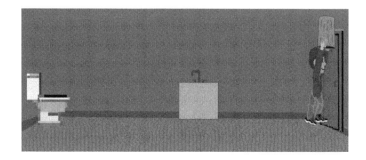

He did not notice it at first, but when he stood up, the rest of our dodgeball group did. Needless to say, there was another riotous chorus of laughter and comments such as "The smell came from you!" It helped that James was not wearing brown shorts.

Fun Fact: Sea turtles are very old organisms. They have been around for more than 220 million years; even outlasting the dinosaurs.

CHAPTER EIGHTEEN

He dashed off to the bathroom and I decided to remain nonchalant. I did not want there to be even the slightest idea that I had hung the trash can from the door. He ran to the door and opened it and there was a loud "Thump" which was followed by yelling and language that I cannot repeat.

The door opened and he stepped out, the trash can still on top of him. He finally got it off with a powerful thrust and then glared at us, he also was shouting, but no one could hear him over the laughter. I cannot say if this was a moment to be proud or ashamed of, but I will say that this bully earned what he got.

Shameless Book Plug: The *Jim Morgan Trilogy* and *Lord of the Wolves* by James Matlack Raney

CHAPTER NINETEEN

A PORTENT OF DANGER

James remained quiet and seemed kind of subdued during dodgeball. He actually spent much of the time standing alone, mainly because he smelled like rotten eggs left marinating in a port-a-potty for a week, ick!

Regarding Dodgeball, the teacher, Mr. Delacruz did not let us play at any real level of

---

Fun Fact: In Elementary School and even in Middle School, we also played a version of Dodgeball we called "Bombardio". Frankly I do not remember it being any different than regular Dodgeball.

intensity, instead choosing to make sure we knew the rules while James Lowes simmered, still hot and angry the trash can incident. So, unlike the day before, it ended without any problems, nor a further visit to the principal.

I was happy to see that those visits had dropped from three the prior day to one and that the intervention of my friends had saved me from any real problems; though I could see that this year and the two following could be a challenge.

I was also delighted that as of yet there was no homework. Marcus had given us great news.

Classic Game Plug: *Realm of Impossibility* (1984) by Electronic Arts is one my favorite computer games. A side-scrolling maze game with spells, zombies, snakes, and other monsters. Check it out sometime!

CHAPTER NINETEEN

He had explained that Tom Harkin Middle School gave very little or no homework, recognizing that youngsters needed time to unwind and that they could burn out if overloaded.

We parted company and I accepted a ride from Bryson's mom to be dropped off since it was on her way. However, she also did my dad and mom a favor; dad had ordered a copy of *Adventures of Huckleberry Finn* from a local bookstore called *Mysterious Galaxy*.

Frankly, I could have spent all day there, but after nearly an hour, we headed home with my

---

Well-deserved plug: *Mysterious Galaxy* is my favorite bookstore. It is located in the Clairemont Area of San Diego. Check them out at www.mystgalaxy.com; you won't be sorry!

copy of the book along with a signed copy of a novel called *Betrayal of the Covenant* by a local writer named Peter Cruikshank, then headed home.

The ride was fun, though Bryson kind of "narc'ed" on me about the events of today, including my two acts of revenge.

MYSTERIOUS GALAXY IS TRULY SAN DIEGO'S FINEST BOOKSTORE!

He winked at me with an "It's all right, she's one of us" looks; it was almost conspiratorial. He

---

Fun Fact: Bryson's real-life mom Terra James is an author of Young Adult fiction. Check out her books online.

was right, she did not give me a disappointed look. Instead she applauded me for my standing up for myself.

"I should not say this, but fire with fire."

I gave a surprised look to hear this from a grownup, but she added "You did not resort to violence, even after that bully punched you. Bravo!"

My home came into view and I dropped the subject. I thanked her for the ride and promised I would look up her books online. Bryson gave me a fist-bump and we "blew it up"

Fun Fact: The video game *Battlezone* (1980) was actually used by the United States Military for training purposes.

and his mom did the same with both of us; yeah, she is totally cool.

I walked into the house which was completely empty. I had not been on my computer in the last few days, so I decided to play a video game or two.

Afterwards, I went onto social media and checked on some of my old friends back home in Mesa, Arizona and sent a few messages and made a post or two. I then began exploring sites about San Diego in general and more particularly, my school.

Video Game Fun Fact: In Pac-Man (1980), the ghosts which pursue him all have different personalities; these personality traits cause them to each pursue Pac-Man in different fashions.

CHAPTER NINETEEN

It was when I looked at names connected to Tom Harkin Middle School that I made a shocking discovery that was a bit alarming; Mike Ripley, James Lowes, and four others at the school were planning to teach me, Bryson, and anyone who was my friend a "painful lesson".

I decided to confront this problem head-on, but how would I do it? Sometimes an answer can be staring you right in the face and you just do not see it. I thought about the right course of action and really had not come up with anything. Then I decided to take a break and read my newest comic book; *Vanguard* – Issue #1; a

---

Fun Fact: Video game company *Atari* was started with an investment of $250.

A PORTENT OF DANGER

comic book filled with masked adventurers (non-powered heroes) who fought crime. An idea came to mind and rather quickly I reached out to Ava, Bryson, Evan, Liam, and Marcus online and told them of my plan all at once.

Classic Game: *Legacy of the Ancients* (1987) is an older RPG game. Your hero could rob local stores for loot, essentially playing the role of an antihero!

PART IV

WE ARE ALL EITHER KINGS OR PAWNS

Fun Fact: Well, fun for me anyways. I spent hours drawing the tennis shoes, so for fun, I kept them on the "King" and "Pawn" drawings of Hugo above.

CHAPTER TWENTY

HELMS MAKES A SPLASH

After about one hour of speaking via computer and telephone, we ended our conniving and I decided to give my eyes a rest. The door downstairs opened and I heard mom come in. I dashed downstairs and she was looking rather pale. Once more, she said she was just not feeling great, but would be ok.

I decided not to share the events of the day with her; I'd tell dad. I mean, he'd probably be

---

(Un)fun Fact: Beloved video game hero Mario is not the hero, but the villain in the game *Donkey Kong Jr.* (1982).

proud that my pranks were a "chip off the old block", right?

Dad came home and he had picked up dinner from a local burger place. We ate quietly and when dad asked about my day, I asked him if I could tell him later and he agreed. Unfortunately, when I did tell him, well he was not angry, but he said he had wished I could have come up with a more constructive way to deal with my problems. He wanted to go down and speak to Principal Nottingham about Mike Ripley hitting me, but I asked him not to. I admit I was disappointed that dad was not impressed with my getting a little payback.

Fun Fact: It's a little-known fact – John Ratzenberger who played *Cliff Clavin* in the TV sitcom *Cheers* had a small role in *The Empire Strikes Back* (1980).

CHAPTER TWENTY

After dinner, I spent a little time watching television with mom and dad, then I walked up to my room and prepared for bed. I grabbed a book and read a little bit and then with my mind wandering towards the day ahead of me for Wednesday, drifted off to sleep.

I awoke early and prepared my backpack for the day. I had plans for me and my friends to contend with Mike Ripley, James Lowes, and the rest of the bullies when they planned their ambush of us. However, I had still more plots for the day, bringing what my dad would call "An equaling out of matters" to school.

Fun Fact: In the comic *Calvin & Hobbes*, the "stuffed tiger" Hobbes is believed to be Calvin's imaginary friend. Series creator Bill Watterson says he is real, but only Calvin can see him.

HELMS MAKES A SPLASH

Mom had made breakfast and seemed energetic and happy. My "Breakfast Supreme" was waiting for me and she had laid out a carafe of hot chocolate (sugar-free of course) to give me that little extra something to face the day.

She sat down with me and we had ourselves a little chat. "Hugo, I know these first two days have been rough, but just be yourself. If you have any problems, tell a teacher you trust or your father and I."

"I promise mom, but the Principal is a n00b. He seems to not like me already and I think he hopes I will get in more trouble."

She paused for a second. I know that parents believe kids are prone to exaggeration, but I

Tsunami Fact: About 80% of tsunamis happen within the Pacific Ocean's "Ring of Fire."

was being truthful. "Hugo, if anything like that happens, tell me. It's not too late to change schools if we need to."

"No mom, I have friends here. I will make it work."

"OK, well your dad's starting the car, why don't you get going. I've got to get ready for work too." She gave me a hug and a kiss and I ran out to dad's car and went to school.

A POSTER FOR NOVEL TASK FORCE: GAEA BY DAVID BERGER ABOVE

Liam joined me at class. He gave me a look of concern. "Are you sure about going through with all your plans today? You could get in a lot of trouble."

Fun Fact: Sharks do not have any bones; they have an entire skeleton made out of cartilage.

HELMS MAKES A SPLASH

"No, I am not sure, but I am going to do it anyways."

"ok then, we've got your back then." To ensure I knew he was serious, he patted my back.

We stepped into Mr. Helms class and he had been standing outside. He gave me a look which I did not understand. It was not spiteful or angry, nor was it friendly. I ignored it and stepped inside. Essentially, he was just greeting all the students as they walked in.

I saw that both Liam and I had our seats now moved to in front of his desk; I guess he wanted to keep an eye on us. This meant that I needed to execute the first stage of my day's plans

---

Fun Fact: There are as many as eighty or more different types of whales in the ocean!

quickly, so I did. The bell rang and Mr. Helms walked in.

As he approached his desk, he saw next to his trash can, a small, chocolate milk carton with the top folded down. This is of course a common trick. You drink the milk, close the carton back up, and then fold the lid over so that it looks like a giant cube. Then you step on it and it makes a loud popping noise.

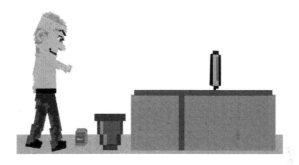

Mr. Helms, perhaps hoping to look cool, raised his leg high and stomped on it hard. However, there was no popping noise, because when I placed it there, I had folded the lid over, but had never emptied the chocolate milk. In fact,

Fun Fact: The computer game *Undertale* has three possible different endings.

HELMS MAKES A SPLASH

I had never opened it, so when he crushed it with his foot, it exploded in a torrent of chocolate milk, all over his slacks, his shoes, his socks, and all over the floor.

The class was likely afraid of Mr. Helms, but that did not stop them, nor me from laughing hysterically. To his credit, he did not shout, nor rant and rave. He merely grabbed a small towel and cleaned it up, but he did not look happy.

Fun Fact: Ok well…fun for me. The "exploding milk carton" trick was popular when I was in school. I successfully pulled it on a few of my friends too.

CHAPTER TWENTY

He did however look at me several times, his face telling me he knew I did it; of course, he could not prove it. I know my dad would not have been proud of me and my mom would have been disappointed. What I did was probably wrong, but I had in my own way sent him a message.

OK, I have no idea what the message was, except maybe to say "I can give as good as I get" and that I hoped would be enough to keep the peace in class.

Never mess with Big Daddy Hugo <EVIL GRIN>

Fun Fact: The Nile River is over 4,100 miles long.

CHAPTER TWENTY-ONE

VANGUARD

The bell rang which dismissed our class and it was time to head for lunch. I had not been scared, but as the time drew near, I felt nervous. Mike Ripley and James Lowes were both a little bigger than me and I had no idea about the four others they engaged to ambush me and my friends.

Fun Fact: There actually are hybrids of lions and tigers. They are called Tigons and Ligers, but they are not a natural breed and sadly do not live healthy lives.

VANGUARD

Still I had committed myself and my friends and we had to make our plan work. Mike Ripley, James Lowes, and his cohorts would be waiting at the juxtaposition of two hallways near the auditorium. I could spot them all waiting in the distance, punching their fists into their hands.

I dashed quickly into the bathroom and opened my backpack and prepared myself. I emerged into the side hall out of the bullies' view and saw my five friends, equally ready and I stifled a chuckle as we looked at each other. Bryson looked at us. "Are we ready to make this school safe from bullies?"

Fun Fact: The Cheetah is the fastest land animal in the world.

CHAPTER TWENTY-ONE

Left to right: Atomic Voice, The Excavator, Freedom Blade, Skunk Girl, Eternal Fire, and Mirth

Evan smiled. "Let's do this!" and this was greeted with a chorus of nods from the rest of us. We stole silently around the other end of the school and approached our quarry carefully. We heard Mike Ripley talking.

"Where are they? I am so ready to give Hugo a knuckle sandwich!" It was incredibly hard not to laugh at them.

Our team of six emerged into view. I said "The only ones who are going to fall are you, you base villains!" Yep, I actually said that, speaking

---

Fun Fact: The Killer Whale is actually a type of dolphin.

VANGUARD

a clichéd comic book line, but it seemed like the thing to say.

"What are you six n00bs supposed to be?" James asked, surprised by our appearance.

Our plan was now revealed. We each were dressed up in hero costumes of the Costumed Adventure team "Vanguard". I had chosen "Mirth", a crimefighter who used joke gadgets to disable the bad guy. Bryson was "Freedom Blade" a brave hero who used a sword and shield, the latter of which he could throw. However,

---

Skunk Fact 1: Skunks eat wasps and honeybees, and will often attack beehives

he had a hardened foam sword from the game "Pit Trade" and a trash can lid as a shield.

BRYSON – AKA "FREEDOM BLADE"

Liam was "Atomic Voice", a skilled crimefighter who used a voice modulator that enabled him to shout loud enough to stun enemies.

Marcus was "Eternal Fire", a scientist who used a flamethrower that could shoot out in a variety of directions. Fearfully enough, he actually had what looked like a flamethrower!

Evan was "The Excavator" who was a crime fighter who had a high-tech shovel and could dig

---

Fun Fact: In 2006, the planet Pluto was demoted to the status of "Dwarf Planet".

big holes. Instead however, he had a regular shovel.

Finally, Ava was "Skunk Girl" whose character in the comic was an Olympic-class gymnast, but carried with her a number of "scent weapons" to beat the bad guys.

AVA - AKA "SKUNK GIRL

"We are Vanguard and we are here to protect the school from you bullies!" Evan said. Our masks may or may not have disguised who we were, but I did not care. I suspected that they knew who we were and honestly did not care one iota.

Skunk Fact 2: A skunk's sulfuric spray has a range of up to 10 feet, and its odor can be detected up to 1.5 miles

CHAPTER TWENTY-ONE

It apparently did not scare them at all those as the six of them came right for us. The first one to find action was Evan. Clay Pagan came at him. Now Evan was on the grass next to the side walk and took a step back. He plunged his shovel hard into it with a lot of force and dislodged a mound of the lawn, leaving a decent-sized hole. Clay lost his footing as his right foot went into the hole and he fell forward and stumbled into the bushes; the Excavator had triumphed!

James Lowes came at Bryson. It happened too quickly for me to help, but Bryson as it turned out did not need any. James tried to punch Bryson in the eye, but Bryson raised up his

---

Fun Fact: it is now believed that there is a massive black hole at the center of the Milky Way galaxy.

shield. It was followed by James clutching his hand...ouch!

Bryson took his sword and swiped it under James' legs and he fell backwards onto the grass.

Luis Alvarez decided to go after Marcus. I worried about this. Would Marcus really bring

---

Fun Fact: The planet Mercury is very hot, with a daytime temperature of over 400 Degrees Celsius!

a flamethrower to school and if so, would he burn Luis to a crisp? Luis drew closer and Marcus raised his weapon and fired...a huge burst of...wait for it...SILLY STRING! It was a LOT of silly string and it was enough to tangle Luis up and impede his movement. Marcus then gave Luis a shove and he fell back on top of James.

That was three down. Rob McIntyre walked slowly and more carefully at Liam. Liam stood there like a statue and I was worried that he was too petrified to fight back. Nope, as Rob got close enough to throw a punch, Liam whipped out a small megaphone and screeched into it. It

---

Fun Fact: During sleep our brains are more active than they are when we are awake.

was strange, but while I heard it, only Rob clutched at his ears. Liam imitated his brother Marcus in shoving the bully onto the grass, on top of his fellows.

Jamie Searles went for Ava. Jamie was probably one of the largest girls in the school. She was nearly six feet tall and had the build of a wrestler. Ava however did not seem concerned. She instead turned her back towards Jamie, squeezed her hands together and I heard a fart noise that was louder than the one I had made the other day after eating the two pizzas.

Fun Fact: The name Dinosaur means "Frighteningly big lizard".

CHAPTER TWENTY-ONE

I am serious, it was deafening! It also smelled awful, like someone dipped a dozen rotten eggs in a swamp! It was, I suppose a replica of the comic book character Skunk Girl's "Stank weapon" and it worked. Jamie turned green and looked nauseous. Ava, just like our other comrades, shoved Karen and she landed atop her bully cohorts with her immense bulk.

Mike Ripley was left and it was clear he knew who I was. "I'm going to loosen all of your teeth."

I was not overly scared. Instead I said calmly "Come get some Captain Brown Pants". He came

---

Fun Fact: Some scientists now believe that even dinosaurs like the Tyrannosaurus Rex may have head feathers! It makes me wonder, did the "T-Rex" taste like chicken?

at me and I used a replica I had made last night of one of Mirth's gadgets; a stink jar. I withdrew it from the pocket of my costume and opened the lid under his nose. The acrid scent reached his nostrils and he staggered back gagging and coughing.

It even made me a little dizzy, but I was determined. I ran forth and gave Mike a shove and he landed atop Karen who had just began to try and rise.

So, there they stood, or laid rather, six bullies defeated by the crime-fighting team of Vanguard. We were indeed a good team, but as

---

Weird Fact: Pinball was illegal from the 1940s to the 1970s in many cities; it was considered a form of gambling. Huh?

CHAPTER TWENTY-ONE

anyone who reads comic books knows, there is always some dissention in the ranks; this one between Skunk Girl and myself.

"My stink weapon is supreme!" I said triumphantly.

"No, mine is!" she said.

This argument went back and forth, but then we each smelled the "aroma" of each other's stink weapon and we began giggling and then smiled at one another. I cannot say for certain, but I think I saw a little cartoon heart appear

---

Fun Fact: The Platypus actually lays eggs, but is a mammal!

above her head; a tiny crush may have indeed been born between us.

Being the leader of the team, I said "Come, let's go to lunch and leave the custodian to dispose of the garbage!"

Fun Fact: The main characters in the game *Contra* were taken from the names of movie actors in the film *Aliens*.

CHAPTER TWENTY-TWO
ARMORED JUSTICE

We left Mike Ripley, James Lowes, and their lackeys lying on the grass, yelling at each other to move their fat carcasses and uttering a number of words I know I didn't use on a regular basis. We still had about fifteen minutes to eat lunch and so we rushed off and grabbed some food (No, I did not buy the pizza).

Fun Fact(?): Spring-Heeled Jack, an entity in English folklore from the 19th century is most-often portrayed in tales as a fiend, but look him up and see what legendary costumed crimefighter he resembles.

ARMORED JUSTICE

We ate quietly, kind of a victory feast celebrating our first foray into the rough-and-tumble world of costumed vigilantes. We spoke a little bit about this not being a one-time act; we could unite to protect our fellow students from the bullies (and maybe a few teachers).

The bell rang and so we threw our trash away and all of us headed for Dr. Raines class, except Marcus who had a different class. We sat down and this time my stomach did not feel bad. He entered the classroom and while all the other students where still chatting, he stopped by my desk and asked if I was feeling better.

Fun Fact: *Hugo Hercules*, a comic strip run from late 1902 to early 1903 is considered the first Superhero comic strip.

CHAPTER TWENTY-TWO

"I did not eat the pizza today sir." He smiled at that and surprised me by extending his fist to me and gave me a fist-bump, which he promptly blew up. I liked this teacher.

"All right class, settle down. A little nonsense is good for the mind, but it is time to get down to brass tacks."

He reached into a large box. When he lifted his arms out, I did see not brass tacks in his hands, but books, about six in each hand. "Hugo, can you and Liam please take these and began handing them out?"

We did as we asked and as we finished, saw that he had another stack. We came and got

---

Fun Fact: Volcanos are actually capable of generating lightning all on their own!

them until the whole class had a copy of the book, *The Adventures of Tom Sawyer*. He commented "We will finish this book within the next two weeks. Go ahead and open to the first page.

I had, as I mentioned already read this book as well as *Adventures of Huckleberry Finn*, but it would be fun to read them again. It was not as cool a book as *Jim Morgan and the King of Thieves*, but there were certainly worse choices of books to read (see book gripe below).

We read for most of the class, taking a few breaks as each student read a paragraph each. The bell rang and Dr. Raines said out loud "For

---

Book Gripe: I love reading, however *The Pearl* and *A Separate Peace* which they made me read in school…ugh!

those of you staying for History, take a quick break to go to the bathroom and be back in your seats in five minutes."

I ran to the bathroom and was stopped by Marcus, who had a worried look on his face. Marcus always had a perpetual smile, so this concerned me. I asked him what was wrong.

"I was about to step into the bathroom and I overheard Ripley and Lowes talking."

I raised my eyebrows. "What did they say?"

"They were plotting a 'costume party' of their own after fifth period for us."

Fun Fact: The Convair F2Y fighter-jet was a unique idea…it was an American seaplane fighter aircraft that rode on twin hydro-skis for takeoff! Yeah. It was a bust.

ARMORED JUSTICE

I frowned. I had not anticipated further problems with them, but I should have. I had to return to class and still needed to use the bathroom. I said "Well, let's suit up after class and take them on."

Marcus seemed sketchy, but then his expression became determined. "Right!"

I excused myself to go pee and then returned to class. Before the bell rang, I quickly let Ava, Evan, Liam, and Bryson know of the plot by our arch-enemies and our plan to foil it. I had expected them to be nervous or apprehensive about it, but no, they were itching for another

Book Plug: Out of the books I was forced to read in school, *The Count of Monte Cristo* and *Huckleberry* are ones I really enjoyed the most.

chance to be heroes, just as we had discussed at lunch.

Dr. Raines got right down to business once the bell rang. He handed history books to everyone.

While this was a United States History class, there was a section on Christopher Columbus and he decided to start there. It was eye-opening as we had always been told Columbus was a great man and it was shocking to find out he was a really bad guy.

With that illusion shattered and the promise by Dr. Raines to shed light on more of our so-called "Historical icons", the bell rang and we

---

Eye-opener: It is this author's opinion that it is disgraceful we honor Christopher Columbus. He was a fiendish, evil man responsible for a number of atrocities.

were dismissed; school was out and the next chapter of our lives as costumed crimefighters was about to begin. I ran to the bathroom and saw that it was empty and once more I assumed the identity of Mirth.

The schoolyard had cleared out quickly and so I emerged from the bathroom in costume and saw my comrades; Skunk Girl, Freedom Blade, Eternal Fire, Atomic Voice, and The Excavator. We walked side-by-side down the main hallway.

As I expected, the bullies were waiting for us, but there was a surprise to this; they were in

Gamer Fact: When the computer game *Maniac Mansion* was released for the Nintendo Entertainment System (NES), the word "Kill" was removed from the title of a video game in the background.

costumes too! Each of them were wearing these black outfits from head to toe, looking like misshapen ninjas. The masks left their face from the nose on down exposed however, so I could tell who was who.

I looked at their costumes and it was almost comical. On the fronts of their shirts were the images of chess pieces. Jamie Searles had the symbol of the Chess Queen, this made sense. However, I laughed at the ones on Mike Ripley and James Lowes' shirts. I mean, I could not believe it, but the other five had pawns!!!

"What a couple of n00bs! You chose to have Pawns as your villain symbol?" I laughed louder

---

Chess Fact: The word "Checkmate" in Chess comes from the Persian phrase "Shah Mat," which means "the King is dead."

and so did my teammates; James and Mike did not. "I guess those ARE appropriate icons to wear though." I said as a dose of verbal venom.

Jamie spoke up for the group, her shirt struggling to retain her bulk without tearing. "This time, it is you who will be lying down in the bushes with more bruises than a bad apple."

Marcus chimed in. "I would ask if you wrote that one, but you'd need to be able to write first." Again, we laughed, they didn't.

The super-fight of the century (or at least the day) was about to begin, but then I heard a crackling noise, like a loose electrical wire was

---

Fun Fact: *Armored Justice* was a planned anti-hero-turned villain in my original *Vanguard* Comic book. When/if I write the novel, he still will be.

exposed nearby. It was followed by a loud thumping noise; it was metal on concrete. I looked and could not believe what I saw.

There, now walking between our two opposing forces, wearing a suit of what appeared to be mechanized armor, with the words "Armored Justice" stenciled on it, was Principal Nottingham!

INTRODUCING..."ARMORED JUSTICE"

ARMORED JUSTICE

"All of you stand down, you have ten seconds to comply!" The voice was cold, harsh, and metallic.

The "battle-suit" WAS intimidating, and perhaps that was part of its problem. The "Chessmen" (which I suppose is a fair name for Jamie Searles' gang of bullies) ran off frantically. I yelled at my friends to do the same, to run and they did. However, as this was my idea, I stayed and allowed myself to be captured.

As he came forward, I removed my mask and revealed myself to be Hugo Finley. Principal Nottingham could not have looked more happy or pleased with himself. "Come with me!" He

---

Fun Fact: Armored Justice's line about having ten seconds to comply is an homage to the 1987 movie *Robocop*.

said triumphantly. My days as a superhero were now over.

Worst costumed hero(?): I would have to say "Arm-Fall-Off-Boy". His arm detached and could be used as a weapon to hit people with. No, I am not making this up.

CHAPTER TWENTY-THREE

HERO FALL

Principal Nottingham glared at me. It was an odd combination of anger and excitement. Of course, he was mad that I had caused all this chaos in his school since my arrival, but he was happy to finally have me in his clutches. So many times he had lost the opportunity to punish me and I was caught red-handed; or was I?

Fun Fact: As a very young kid, my mom would use a pair of clothespins to fasten a towel to my shirt. I then pretended to be a hero whom I called "Lightning Man".

HERO FALL

"I am really tired of having you in my office, what is this, the fourth time?" he asked, barely concealing his enjoyment of the moment.

"Fifth, but this is the fifth time I've done nothing wrong!" I answered with a surprising amount of defiance in my tone. I was mad. What had Principal Nottingham done to quell the bullies? Nothing, and I wanted to be sure he knew it.

"I believe you used some kind of stink bomb during lunch, that is a major infraction." He said, obviously losing his temper.

"I do not recall doing any such thing." I answered, lying of course, but I reasoned that

Shameless Book Plug: Peter Cruikshank's *Dragon-Called* series.

CHAPTER TWENTY-THREE

I needed to protect myself and my friends (and their identities).

"Well, let me see your belt." He pointed at my "Mirth Belt" as I called it. I smiled at him and he was taken aback as I handed it to him with no hesitation.

He opened up the variety of pouches to find...erasers, a mini-pencil sharpener, breath mints, and a pack of tooth floss (hygiene is important kids), and a six-sided die.

Parental Advice: It's no joke, your teeth are the best friends you have. Take care of them now and avoid a lot of cavities and toothaches later.

HERO FALL

"As you can see sir, I carried no such thing as a stink bomb, my belt pouches have no such room." In truth, of course it was not a bomb, but rather something I made at home in a jar.

The jar itself had mud, pepper, vinegar, and other things I had left out overnight and had a really putrid smell. Despite that however, it was not a stink bomb and I had thrown it away after its one use; hey I didn't want to smell it either.

Fun Fact: The stink jar is loosely based on a true story. In the fifth grade, I put ice, dirt, water, vinegar, pepper, and other stuff from the kitchen in a jar and left it overnight. I cannot remember all of the ingredients, but when I took it for "Show and Tell", the stink made the other kids' eyes water and their noses wrinkle up.

CHAPTER TWENTY-THREE

Nottingham looked disappointed. There was no rule in dressing up like a hero and he had done the same thing to confront us. I had to wonder; what in the world was HE doing with a costume? I mean really, a MECHA battle-suit? Actually, that would be cool, if he wasn't such a nOOb!

"Dismissed" he said, and he sighed, looking almost like a balloon with the air let out of it. I was relieved that he had not chosen to ask who my comrades were. He could punish me if he were to ask and I refused, but so far, so good.

I left his office and as fortune would have it I heard a honk and it was Liam and Marcus with

---

Fun Fact: Dental floss can be used to cut cheese. Huh heh, I said cut cheese...tee hee hee!

their dad in the car. "Come on Hugo, dad will give you a ride home."

The ride to my house was interesting. Liam and Marcus took turns telling the story of our "battle against evil", which I suppose it was. Their dad, far from looking angry or disappointed was excited. He actually made what I thought was a surprising, but cool comment.

"When I was about your age, I did some hacking with my computer. At least your antics were productive and helpful."

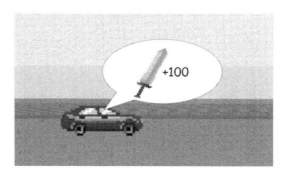

Fun Fact: True story; Liam and Marcus' father in real-life did hack into a videogame called *Wizardry* to give his main warrior a +100 sword.

CHAPTER TWENTY-THREE

I got home and reflected on the downside of today's events; my career as a crimefighter was over and I would need to hang up my costume.

Fun Fact: The Bermuda Triangle affects compasses so that they do not point true north. This is why so many ships and planes have gotten lost inside of it.

CHAPTER TWENTY-FOUR

A RISING STORM

Mom was again not feeling her best when I got home. She told me she was just a bit dizzy and for the umpteenth time told me not to worry. It had been a bit hot this last week, so maybe this was getting to her.

Of course, we had spent the last decade or more in Arizona where it was infinitely hotter,

---

Fun Fact: The title of this chapter is a loose homage to the 1986 technothriller novel *Red Storm Rising* by Tom Clancy.

but here in San Diego, we had less heat, but more humidity. Was this why? I promised not to worry, but a concern for her remained in the back of my head.

Dr. Raines had sent us home with a little homework. We were to read up on Mark Twain and write a one-paragraph report on him. Also for our United States History class, we were to read up on any American historical figure and write out a one-paragraph report on him or her as well.

I went upstairs and using the Internet found a plethora of facts on Mark Twain and then studied Abraham Lincoln, the sixteenth President of the United States.

Fun Fact: Abraham Lincoln was a lawyer, but did not have a law degree.

CHAPTER TWENTY-FOUR

The phone rang and I answered it; it was Ava.

"Hi Skunk Girl, how are you?" She laughed.

"Hey Mirth, what are you up to?" She asked.

"Finishing Dr. Raines' homework, why, what's up?"

"My mom got me tickets to the Laser bowling at the Volcano Alley, six of them. Two free games each. I wanted to see if you, Liam, Marcus, and Bryson wanted to go with Evan and I?"

"Sure, that would be awesome!" I said probably a little TOO excitedly. I prayed it

Fun Fact: The name "Volcano Alley" is an homage to the "Clairemont Bowl" bowling alley, near where I grew up that had a nightclub called "*The Volcano Club*".

A RiSiNG STORM

would not sound like a crush, but I really wanted to go bowling and it was cool that Ava asked me.

She giggled and said "Seven O'clock till nine o'clock this evening, you'll be there?"

I explained I would ask my parents and I reluctantly bothered mom who I was glad to see had again regained her energy and now sitting with her laptop out and cheerfully typing away. When I asked, she smiled without concern said she would be delighted to take me. I gave her a concerned look, but she assured me (again) there was nothing to worry about.

Fun Fact: The first season of the television sitcom *Gilligan's Island* was filmed in Black and White, the remaining seasons were done in color.

CHAPTER TWENTY-FOUR

We got in the car and she drove me there. I arrived and was excited to be greeted by Liam and Marcus. We said hello and we walked inside and there was Bryson, Evan, and Ava getting their "rent-a-shoes." I got mine and we all found our lane. Then we went walking along the rows to look for a bowling ball for each of us; which is always an adventure.

As we did, I saw a few familiar faces and they were not ones that I was happy to see. Mike Ripley, James Lowes, and Jamie Searles were bowling too and as it turned out, they had picked their balls and the only lane left was next to ours.

Fun Fact: In bowling, the 7-10 split is considered the hardest one to pick up. However, statistically some say the 4-6-7 split is even harder.

A RISING STORM

James saw who his new lane neighbors were and laughed. "Looks like there is a lane for losers in this alley." They each laughed knowing that we were not about to start trouble, but that door swings both ways.

"It figures you'd enjoy bowling, anything with a gutter to remind you and your friends of home." I said.

"You got a smart mouth n00b and I'm going to shut it for you the next time we're alone." Mike said. "The next punch in the mouth will loosen a tooth or too."

Fun Fact: Over 8 Billion cans of SPAM have been sold worldwide!

"Whatever." I said, feeling the butterflies rise in my stomach, the old "fight or flight" feeling taking hold. I was a bit nervous, but I would remain cool.

Ava stepped over. "Since you are big in talk, maybe you'd like to have a little wager on our games tonight?"

James looked a bit embarrassed and said "I'd love to, I know we'd mop the floor with you, but I have no extra money."

Fun Fact: Not recommending this, but pinball machines are very easy to "tilt". As kids, my brother and I would walk by and just push hard on the front to tilt them.

A RISING STORM

"Good, then the losers have to write the word n00b since you like it so much, on their forehead with a permanent marker at school tomorrow."

Jamie chimed in. "You're on!"

I had wished that she had not suggested this. I am an ok bowler, but not great; I mean I consider breaking 100 points to be a fair game. We decided that since there were six of us and three of them, we would take up three lanes and their average total score would have to beat ours as a six-person team. I gulped at the thought, honestly believing we were doomed.

Fun Fact: There is a San Diego city in the state of Texas.

CHAPTER TWENTY-FOUR

The game started and Ava and Evan apparently had played a lot as they both got strikes. I knocked down seven pins total on the first frame. Jamie then began and rolled a perfect strike, but the floor buzzed; she had crossed the line. Mike then saw a repeat of Jamie's misfortune, with the same buzz. This was odd, I saw that he had remained behind the line. James also stayed behind the line and got a strike, but the computer registered only five pins.

The game continued on. Jamie and her two toadies continued to out-bowl us as a team, but

Fun Fact: Despite being over 25 years old, there are still new games being released for the *Sega Genesis* game system.

A RiSiNG STORM

the scores did not bear that out and they were becoming quite frustrated. Then I saw why.

Kristoffer, the center-fielder from my baseball team was sitting there with a laptop and snickering each time Jamie's team bowled; he was hacking the lane's sensors and the scoreboard's computer. Jamie's team was slaughtering us, but of course, according to the scoreboard, we were destroying them. I said nothing, finding it funny.

Fun Fact: I am a lousy bowler, but my oldest brother has rolled numerous 300 games.

CHAPTER TWENTY-FOUR

If I had expected Jamie, Mike, or James to own up to their loss (invalid though it was), I was of course to be disappointed. They never figured out why the scores were not reflecting their actual performance, but they were not about to accept a loss to us, deserved or not.

"We'll settle this another time." Mike said, and the three of them left.

"Well at least we spoiled their night, eh?" Kristoffer said, walking over, holding his laptop up as if it were a trophy.

Fun Fact: Most of the actors who played main characters in *Star Trek* also appeared in at least one episode of *The Twilight Zone*.

A RISING STORM

We all laughed and as the night ended, I reflected on the week so far. Three days in and they had been rather eventful, but I would learn soon that I had seen nothing yet.

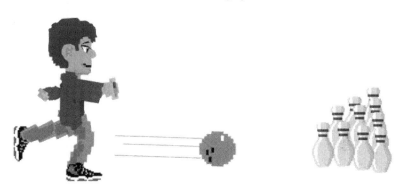

Fun Fact: Jack Klugman and Burgess Meredith are tied for the most appearance in *The Twilight Zone*.

PART V

BATTLES FOR LIFE AND DEATH!

Fun Fact: In the video arcade game *NBA Jam*, you can unlock a free tank game; even without inserting a token or quarter to play it.

CHAPTER TWENTY-FIVE

THE RUNNING DEAD

My dad had picked me up and took me home. I did not tell him about the details of my evening, but merely told him bowling went well. He was glad that I had enjoyed a good night and said he had been worried about the rough week I'd had.

Well, I assured him things would improve, though I was not convinced. It was nearly ten o'clock when we got home, so I ran upstairs, put on my pajamas, brushed my teeth and then went to bed; I was asleep in moments.

Fun Fact: In the movie *Raiders of the Lost Ark* (1981), the droids R2-D2 and C3PO from the *Star Wars* movie saga make an appearance...as hieroglyphics...twice!

THE RUNNING DEAD

The next morning I awoke, excited to head to my Journalism class and see what she thought about my article. I did not really believe her when she said that my article on "Fun, but harmless pranks" had possibilities, but still wanted to see what she thought about my writing. Beyond that, I had another idea for an article based on my brief foray into the superhero world the day before.

Ava and Bryson were in class waiting for me when I arrived and they each were already

---

Tsunami Fact: Up to one-half hour before a tsunami strikes, the ocean can suddenly appear to drain away. This recession of the water is called "Drawback" and is a good indicator that you should flee to higher ground.

pounding away at their keyboards. Ava was writing an article about classic computer games, mentioning titles that came out decades before she was born. I saw her mention the title *Mail Order Monsters* which I thought was an odd title for a game, but had to assume it was good if she was writing about it.

Bryson was writing an interesting article called "The Mentos Experiment" which was the results of him placing the popular candy in a variety of different diet sodas and charting how high the soda shot out of the bottle. I had

---

Fun Fact: *Mail Order Monsters* is a 1985 computer game published by *Electronic Arts*. Odd title or not, it is an amazing game with unlimited replay value and definitely a classic!

never tried it, but wanted to read his results when he was done so I could try it.

The bell rang and Lady Pain dropped off each of our articles from Tuesday. She had made a few corrections on mine, mainly pointing out word repetition and a few grammatical errors and a small note at the bottom that said "Consider this for a monthly article on pranks".

This surprised me, but of course it also had me excited as my dad would also have some fun helping me with this. She then asked us to come

---

Fun Fact: The Mentos Experiment really works. Drop one into a bottle of diet soda and stand back, it's fun!

up with a second article, this one related to our school. I became even more excited as this assignment was perfect aligned with my desire to write about me and my friends' defeat of the bullies during lunch yesterday as *Vanguard*.

I knew Principal Nottingham would soon write some kind of notice or have the teachers speak about our actions as deplorable, but this article would allow me to defend our team, though of course I would write of us without revealing the identity of me or my fellow crimefighters.

Fun Fact: Speaking of Vanguard, it is also the name of a classic 1981 multi-scrolling, multi-directional arcade game.

THE RUNNING DEAD

The article practically wrote itself and before I knew it, I had written six pages and the bell was ringing. Ava, Bryson, and I went to lunch and this time, it was uneventful. I saw James Lowes and the rest of the bullies, but they ignored me, so we had a safe lunch.

Fourth period Pre-Algebra was equally without any problems. It was a relatively boring class, but at least without the rancor between me and Mike Ripley who did not even look in my direction. I thought maybe he had learned his

---

Fun Fact: Nitroglycerin is one of the most explosive materials in the world, but is also used to save the lives of someone having a heart attack. I should know, it saved mine.

lesson, but I knew better. Someday, sometime, he would try and exact his revenge.

The bell rang for sixth period and I got halfway to the gymnasium when I realized I left my backpack in class. I returned to Mr. Lawhead's room and retrieved it. Mr. Delacruz reminded me to be less forgetful in the future. He then told me to change into my gym clothes and join the class on the dirt field.

I changed, wondering why we were not going to the gymnasium for dodgeball, but then

---

Tsunami Fact: It is believed that 3.5 billion years ago, a meteorite struck the Earth. The resulting tsunami is believed to have wiped out all life on the planet!

overheard that the custodian had waxed the floor and it was too slippery to play, but that there was a rather unusual surprise for the sixth period students on the dirt field outside.

I left the locker room and walked outside and turned the corner onto the dirt field and could not believe what I saw. Bryson was there, a look of terror in his eyes. I saw the source of his fear; he was being chased...by a zombie!

I always assumed that zombies walked or lurched like Frankenstein's monster. However,

---

Fun Fact: Frankenstein was the name of the doctor who created Frankenstein's monster. The monster itself was not called Frankenstein, though it is often incorrectly referred to by that name.

there were a dozen of them and they were all running; not fast, but running, and they did not seem to be tiring out too much. Bryson was a quick runner, but as luck would have it, he tripped and fell hard onto the dirt field and the zombie began moving in for the kill.

At that moment, I admit I wished that I'd had my Mirth costume on, but I did not. No, if I was to help my friend, it would be as plain, normal Hugo Finley. I waited a second as Bryson turned on the oval dirt track and then the zombie began to follow suit.

Unwritten rule of zombie survival: Be faster than the slowest runner.

THE RUNNING DEAD

At this point, still unseen, I ran forward as fast as I could and at the last moment, I leapt forward in what could best be described as a flying tackle. I collided with the zombie, my shoulders striking it in the midsection and my arms wrapping around it. I heard an "Oomph!" sound come from him as I struck him and we both landed in the dirt, hard.

"Hey! What's the big idea of tackling me kid?"

Uh-oh, I may have made a big mistake. I raised my head and saw that a whole field full of people were looking at me.

Fun Fact: There are hybrids of Polar Bears and Grizzly Bears; they are called "Grolar Bears" and "Pizzly Bears".

CHAPTER TWENTY-FIVE

I stammered "I thought you were a zombie and were going to eat my friend's brains?" I said, feeling really stupid now.

"Hugo, this is a zombie run!" Bryson said, his face still sweaty, but not looking scared. "We were invited to join it because our gym can't be used."

I looked at the adult in his zombie makeup who began laughing at me. I then saw there was an adult who was not laughing; it was Principal Nottingham. He did not even say anything, but merely beckoned me with his hands to follow him...to his office...again. *Sigh*

Fun Fact: The first zombie movie was the 1932 film *White Zombie* starring Bela Lugosi of *Dracula* (1931 film) fame.

CHAPTER TWENTY-SIX

AFTERMATH

I could say with some confidence that the chair that I sat on in Nottingham's office was "my traditional seat." How many times this week had I sat in it already? This time I was certain I would be placed in detention or perhaps even suspended. He of course looked delighted to finally have me where he could exact some discipline upon me after I had escaped his clutches several times.

I awaited the worst from him, but became startled when the door opened and a police

---

Fun Fact: George Washington in fact did NOT have wooden teeth. His false teeth were made from ivory and sometimes human teeth purchased from others.

AFTERMATH

officer came in; was I being arrested? He came over and took a seat next to me.

"Principal Nottingham, I think you should let this kid go. I'm not hurt," (he looked at me sideways) "though that was quite a nice hit you gave me." He turned his gaze back. "I learned from Coach Delacruz that he was late to the field and so did not know about his class being asked to join the zombie run as runners."

Principal Nottingham looked crestfallen, but did not seem prepared to let me go without an argument.

Fun Fact: The most venomous animal in the world is not a snake or a spider, but the Box Jelly, sometimes incorrectly called the "Box Jellyfish".

CHAPTER TWENTY-SIX

"Principal Nottingham, he may have acted impulsively, but he was trying to save his friend. He was foolish, but heroic and I think he should be commended." He then extended his fist to me and we "blew it up" and I admit a wave of relief fell over me.

"Ok, Finley, return to class, but I do not want to see you in my office again this week!"

Well then hey, why did he keep bringing me in here then? I looked around to see if I had said that out loud, but fortunately I did not. "Thank

---

(Un)Fun Fact: Nintendo licensed their Zelda series for the CD-i video game console; it became infamous as one of the worst uses of a video game license ever.

AFTERMATH

you." I said to both the officer and nodded at Principal Nottingham and left to return to class.

How time flies though, I mean the bell rang before I even got there. So, as everyone was leaving school, I was in the locker room changing back into my regular clothes. This was what military men and women would refer to as a "tactical mistake". The reason being was that I was alone in the locker room.

Bullies I think must have some kind of predatory sense, because I found myself alone, surrounded by Mike Ripley, James Lowes, and

Tsunami Fact: The 1960 Valdivia Earthquake off the coast of Chile is the largest earthquake ever recorded. Within thirty minutes, waves of over 80 feet in height struck the coast!

Jamie Searles. Their three cohorts were not with them, but it was still three-to-one odds and I knew that they were not in my favor. Still, I was prepared to go down fighting.

"Relax n00b." Jamie said. "Delacruz is in the other room; we aren't going to beat you down here."

"Ok then, where and when? I assume you are trying to schedule a fight."

"Tonight, but I suggest a different way to settle this, one where you can't cheat."

Fun Fact: The difference between venom and poison: Poison is absorbed or ingested, venom is injected via bites, stings, spurs, etc.

AFTERMATH

"I'm listening, what do you propose?"

"Tonight, Action City Miniature Golf Course is closing early, eight o'clock. Meet us there and we'll have a little competition."

"You want to play miniature golf against us on a closed course?" I asked, a bit confused.

"No, bring your nerd friends. It will be six-on-six in a game of *Lazer Storm*, I assume you DO have a Lazer Storm gun like anyone cool does, don't you?"

Fun Fact: The first ever video game "Easter Egg" is believed to be in the 1979 Atari videogame *Adventure*. In a hidden area is text giving credit to the game's creator.

CHAPTER TWENTY-SIX

"Of course I do, we'll see you there!" Actually, I did not, and I had no idea if my friends did, but I wanted to settle this, even if the whole idea of playing some kind of wargame against these jerks seemed stupid; oh, and illegal as well.

Dad picked me up and told me that him and mom needed to speak to me before bed that night, but there was nothing to worry about. He did not know about the "Zombie Apocalypse" at school. I then hit him up for a favor.

"Dad, tonight there is a *Lazer Storm* game held at Action City Miniature Golf Course after

---

Fun Fact: Speaking of Easter Eggs, the first arcade game believed to have one is the 1976-77 game *Starship 1*. In it, the player can trigger the message "Hi Ron!"

hours. The only problem is I don't have a kit for the game.

"How much are they?" he asked me and I winced as I prepared to answer.

"Forty dollars I think." I was so certain he was going to say no.

"Well, that's a bit expensive, but you've had a rough week and you need to blow off a little steam, so let's go get it now."

I did not tell dad that my Lazer Storm game would be on a closed grounds and that I would

---

Fun Fact: The game of *Laser Tag* was inspired by the film *Star Wars (1977)*.

be trespassing and so would my friends. Dad had taken me to a local department store and bought me the "Epic Lazer Storm Rifle Kit". It also came with a pistol which I thought I might need; you never know.

I got home and managed to reach each of my friends and they all jumped at the opportunity. We really wanted to beat these guys that badly. I got dressed in a pair of black jeans and a black t-shirt, and then dad took me to what I would refer to as the "warzone".

Fun Fact: The Washington National Cathedral has a Darth Vader gargoyle. It's true…look it up!

CHAPTER TWENTY-SEVEN

BATTLE CRY

We arrived in the parking lot at about the same time. I was worried that dad might spot Jamie, Mike, and James and wonder why I was playing games with bullies, but then I remembered; he would not recognize them and they were not there waiting for us. I assumed they would be inside the park, maybe doing some reconnaissance.

Dad left me with my friends and as soon as all our parents had departed, James, Mike, Jamie,

---

Fun Fact: The 1938 radio play War of the Worlds was believed to have caused a nationwide panic that Earth was under assault from alien invaders. This belief has since been largely discounted as untrue or at least, exaggerated.

and the other three showed themselves. Security appeared also and began ushering people to the exit, but we all made as if we were friends waiting for our families to pick us up, which was kind of true; except for the part about us all being friends.

Soon enough the lights went out inside the arcade and on the rides, leaving only sparse lighting on the golf courses. Several more minutes passed and we were all alone. James stepped forward.

"Ok, here's the deal. There are three golf courses, Wild West, Intercontinental, and Fairy

---

Don't "Turnip" your nose at this, but... Jack-o'-lanterns were once made out of turnips, beets and potatoes...not pumpkins

CHAPTER TWENTY-SEVEN

Tale. We'll start in Fairy Tale, your team starts in Wild West. I will give a shout when it is time to begin."

He cleared his throat and began fastening on his head and chest sensors. "In case none of you n00bs have played, a hit on any sensor will cause it to buzz loudly, there will be no doubt that you have been eliminated. The last team with a player not killed wins."

"So ok, what are the stakes?" Evan asked, somewhat boldly.

Fun Fact: This golf course is loosely based on where I had my first job. They had a Western, International, and Storybook course.

BATTLE CRY

"If we win, you (he pointed at me) will get a daily punch in the arm every day for the next month! If you win, we'll leave you alone and stop hacking on you."

"Not good enough!" Ava said. She reached into her bag and withdrew a pink belt with unicorns sewn into it. "If we win, then you have to wear this pink girdle at school tomorrow, AND stop being mean to my friends!"

"No deal!" James shouted

"Actually, you are right." Ava said, pulling out another girdle, the twin of the one she had

---

Fun Fact: This is loosely based on truth; sort of. My dad and his friends would go camping every summer. They had a contest each year and the loser wore the pink girdle on their arm when they went into town for breakfast.

shown James. "Mike, you have to wear this too if we win. It's that or you can count on us dishing out our own unique brand of punishment for the rest of the school year."

"No, that's stupid! I'm calling this off and tomorrow when I find you alone..."

Jamie chimed in. "It's a deal! James, Mike, don't be a couple of wimps! It's obvious that they've never played this before. We'll take them out in ten minutes and then take turns

---

Fun Fact: This event is also loosely based on true facts. At my first job at a miniature golf course, we would play *Lazer Tag* on all three golf courses and play until the sun came up.

punching Hugo in the arm for the rest of the year."

"Fine!" James said, though his voice quavered with anticipation.

Jamie led her charges off and I followed Ava and the rest over to the Wild West course. It was not too much later when they heard the shout "It's go time!"

Marcus spoke quietly. "Hugo, you have the rifle. Liam, Bryson, and I will move quietly over

Fun Fact: In the 2003 video game *Max Payne 2: The Fall of Max Payne*, you can enter a room that has a memorial to Miika Forssell, a developer who died during the making of the game.

CHAPTER TWENTY-SEVEN

to Intercontinental. We will move slowly, but leave ourselves as bait, getting them to shoot at us. We'll stay near cover so it will be more likely that they will miss. When they fire, you'll see their guns light up and you take them out, got it?"

"I got it, but what about Ava and Evan?" I asked.

"We'll stay back and keep in reserve, but also watch to see if we spot them. If we do, we'll try and sneak around and get them too. Agreed?"

Shameless Book Plug: The *Black Bead Chronicles* by J. D. Lakey

BATTLE CRY

It seemed a good plan to all of us, so we quietly said "Agreed" in unison and Liam, Marcus, Bryson, and I began moving off. The three of them moved ahead of me at a slightly faster rate. As for me, I chanced upon a perfect "sniper's nest"; an imitation Bavarian castle with a moat in front of it.

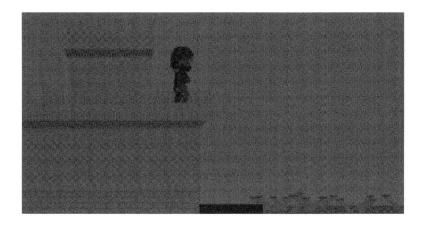

At first, I considered using the top of the castle as a perfect spot to sit and pick off Jamie and her underlings, but I realized the laser would give me away and then I'd be a sitting duck.

Grave fact: A graveyard adjoins a church, a cemetery does not. Also, you cannot busy ashes in a graveyard. Of course, let us all stay healthy as long as possible ok?

Then I heard the sound of someone coming. I needed to hide and quickly, so I climbed reluctantly down into the moat, first hurriedly removing my head and chest gear so they would not get ruined. The water smelled rather badly and it was cold, but at the same time, it was dark and unlit so I remained unseen.

The unknown combatant turned out to be Clay Pagan, one of Jamie's cohorts. He was doing a fair job of skulking about. I had been fortunate to hear him, and if he had not been murmuring about something, he might've snuck right up on me.

Fun Fact: The bricks for the pyramids were cut with saws; some of them still retain the marks!

BATTLE CRY

He then did something that nearly gave me away as I had to restrain myself from laughing. He apparently had to go to the bathroom, as he turned away from the moat and began peeing on a nearby bush. Needless to say, he dropped his gun. My gun of course was out of the water, but hidden behind the reeds I was camouflaged in, which obscured me quite well. Though sadly not my view of what Clay was doing...*sigh*.

Clay REALLY had to go as he kept going for nearly a minute. I decided to be a nice guy and let him finish. Once he did though, I fired at his sensor. His kit buzzed loudly and he spun

---

(Un)Fun Fact: Castles did not have toilets, but "Garderobes" which emptied into the moats. As you may guess, castles smelled pretty bad in the old days.

around; fortunately he had managed to zip up first, though he had of course not washed his hands.

"What the...?!? Who shot me?" He shouted.

I did not need to tell him, and I suspected that if I did, he'd find a way to reveal my position, so I said nothing, but quietly lowered myself back down into the reeking water. I will give him credit for one thing; he did not argue, he acknowledged he was the first kill and walked out of the golf course. The current score was Vanguard 1, Chessmen 0.

Tsunami Fact: Don't try to swim against a tsunami, it is too powerful. Instead try to find an object and hold on as you are carried by the current.

CHAPTER TWENTY-EIGHT
REVERSED FORTUNE

They say that no battle plan survives contact with the enemy. I am not sure if that is true, but in this case it was. I clambered out of the water, shivering like crazy, but happy that I had scored the first kill of the contest. This would change shortly.

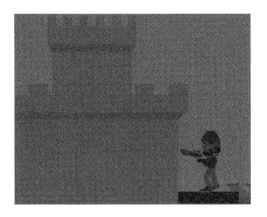

Bryson came into the corner of my view. He was moving quite stealthily, He stayed in the dark which matched his own dark green shirt and dark gray pants. His pistol was also covered

---

Baseball Fact: A batter who is hit by a pitch, even if he did not swing at it, is not automatically given first base; the umpire can rule that he did not try to dodge it. In that case, it would likely just be called a ball.

with what looked like a black argyle sock; hey, it did the job.

He was creeping along the outside of the castle, again this was clever as he was moving amongst the shadows. However, fate did not look kindly down upon him. One of the lights nearby that had appeared to be off...well apparently it had not been, it had simply not been working. It chose that moment to light up and Bryson was perfectly silhouetted against the wall.

I learned then that one of their teams also had a rifle like mine. Bryson's sensor buzzed

Fun Fact: In the video game *Force Unleashed* (2008), you can find generally despised character *Jar Jar Binks* frozen in Carbonite.

loudly. I was only ten feet away from him and he did not see me. The rules stated that since he was dead, I could not talk to him, otherwise I'd have at least let him know it was a tough break. Also, he might've tipped me off where the sniper was.

Liam was the next one to get waxed. He had also been sneaky, but he stumbled just a tad going over the wall and got tagged by the sniper. However, this time, I saw the light from the rifle in the distance. I had a brief window of opportunity to shoot him if I was lucky.

Fun Fact: An item in a film noir movie used to drive the story and advance the plot is called a MacGuffin. A perfect example is the Maltese Falcon in the movie...yep, you guessed it...*The Maltese Falcon* (1941).

REVERSED FORTUNE

I put the scope up to my eye and aimed, but I could not see the exact spot. I COULD of course fire blindly, but it would reveal my position; no, I would need to wait and see if he fired again regretfully.

Marcus must have guessed the situation I was in. He exposed himself to the sniper, but having seen Liam get it, he quickly dodged back. He therefore was not hit, but I saw the brief blip of the laser and that was all I needed. I fired and was glad to hear evidence that the 300 foot range advertised on the box was not a lie.

Fun Fact: Automobile designer Preston Tucker once built a tank for the U. S. Military in 1938. One reason it was allegedly not purchased was that it actually could move too fast.

CHAPTER TWENTY-EIGHT

The buzzing went off and echoed across the course. The sniper was gone and I had the satisfaction of seeing Mike Ripley climb down from his hiding spot above a brick wall.

Luck was still on my side, or rather stupidity was. Luis and Rob both emerged from cover and began asking Mike where I was; which was of course against the rules. I tagged Luis with a perfect shot. Luis looked up at me and saw that I got him.

Fun Fact: As the illustrations above indicate, Mysterious Galaxy is my favorite bookstore, excuse my shameless plug. BTW, some of my books are on their shelves.

REVERSED FORTUNE

However, the buzzing of his sensor was competing with Rob's own sensor as Marcus came out from behind cover and shot him, the sensor on his head seeming to rattle Rob's teeth.

I then heard a buzzing from the Wild West area. Liam and I joined up. Now this was foolish; if there were other members of Jamie's team nearby, he or she could've killed us both in seconds.

Luckily fortune favored the foolish, no one shot at us; this meant likely that Jamie and James had gone over to the Wild West area. I turned to Marcus and whispered "We better get over there."

Fun Fact: Cartoon character *Yosemite Sam* has a real name; it is Samuel Michelangelo Rosenbaum.

CHAPTER TWENTY-EIGHT

We both skulked quietly over there, moving patiently and keeping carefully to the darkness. It turned out when we came closer that Evan and Jamie had both been shot. I could hear them talking amongst themselves. Evan had nailed Jamie and James had apparently nailed Evan. This meant the odds were still three-to-one in our favor. Ava fired at someone in the distance, but heard no buzzing to indicate a hit. She looked back and forth for her elusive target, but did not spy him.

The odds changed quickly. James suddenly popped up, actually from only a dozen or so feet

---

Fun Fact: There was a prehistoric sloth known as the ground sloth, which is now extinct. It could reach over fifteen feet in height!

in front of her and eliminated her. He had actually emerged from a box. I would later learn that he had dashed by her and she had indeed shot at him. However, he had crept down a utility ladder and ran under the course and then emerged to shoot her. Clever, but of course this meant that he had knowledge of the course. He had probably competed in this contest before here.

What he had not taken into account of however, was that there were still a pair of us left and he had rather loudly revealed his

---

Fun Fact: Look at Mario from the *Mario Bros.* games; his blue coveralls? They are the aliens from the arcade game *Space Invaders!*

location. Moreover, he was rather absorbed in letting Ava know she had been eliminated. In fact, he was so distracted, that he did not notice Marcus as he casually walked over to him and from just a few feet away pulled the trigger.

James leapt impressively high when the sensor's buzzing surprised him. I swear the animatronic vulture said "You got zapped n00b!", but it may have just been my imagination.

When James landed, his face was so red, he nearly glowed in the dark it seemed. Then I

Did they surf? Mastodons, an extinct, distant relative to the modern elephant existed in Southern California. They died out over 10,000 years ago.

realized it was not his face that was glowing, but the light of a siren.

Fun Fact: The hole in the pull tab on a soda can is so you can turn it around and place a straw through it.

PART I

T
G
I
F

Fun Fact: The Nintendo Entertainment System game *River City Ransom* used music from the game *Double Dragon* in the final, climatic boss battle.

CHAPTER TWENTY-NINE
IT'S FRIDAY, FRIDAY

Friday

The next morning, I awoke feeling as if I had not slept for more than a few minutes. In actuality, that was not far from the truth; I had slept only four or five hours instead of my usual nine or ten. Today, I knew would be a long day, but at least it was Friday.

The twelve of us had been fortunate. The siren was not from a police car, but from a

---

Book Plugs: The posters in the drawing above are *Dragon Lad: Tale of the Talisman* by JC Stevens and *The Dangerous Christmas Ornament* by Bob Siegel.

roving security vehicle who had the park as one of the stops on his route. The general manager of Action City had been called and had thought the whole matter funny, though he was equally relieved that no one had been hurt and no damage done.

The guard had arranged for our parents to pick us all up. Dad and mom had not been thrilled at the phone call and the ride home had been quiet, but if I thought that the night's events had been exciting, it was nothing compared to when I got home.

Fun Fact: Leonardo da Vinci drew up plans for a robot in 1495.

CHAPTER TWENTY-NINE

They sat me down and dad immediately started in on me. "Hugo, I am surprised at you! I hope you will set a better example for your baby brother!"

I gave a puzzled look. "What baby brother?"

It was then that mom and dad dropped the bombshell on me. Mom was going to have another baby; this was why she had not been feeling well. They wanted me to get through the first week of school before telling me, but I guess this seemed like the better time; using it was a teachable moment.

Baseball Fact: In 1956, New York Yankee pitcher Don Larsen pitched the first and (thus far) only Perfect Game in World Series history.

iT'S FRiDAY, FRiDAY

I was really excited and happy. I had always wanted a little brother, even though I would be quite a bit older than him. The other good thing about this was that in all the joy and excitement, dad and mom decided not to punish me, but instead said that no matter how tired I was, I would be going to school the next day. That reminder was with me throughout the morning as I got dressed and splashed water on my face to try and wake myself up with limited success.

As I arrived at school and was greeted by my friends (also looking quite tired), we all remembered that no one had given James the

---

Fun Fact: The deepest part of the ocean is called the "Challenger Deep"; it reaches a depth of over 35,000 feet!

pink girdle and we all agreed that he would likely welch on our contest. We had won, but it was a hollow victory since we had deceived ourselves if we thought anything would change; they would still be bullies and we were all the more sleepless for our efforts.

Liam and I entered Mr. Helms class and I checked under my desk and all around it for any sign that he might have plotted some kind of revenge. Hey, even paranoids have enemies.

If there was something there, I did not see it. Liam and I were both surprised (and relieved) to see that Mr. Helms remained neutral towards us

---

Yawn: Koalas can sleep up to 18 hours per day!

iT'S FRiDAY, FRiDAY

for the nearly one hour of class. Friday of course is all six classes, about fifty-five minutes each, so you get the best (and worst) of all worlds.

Second period went well, Lady Pain loved the article on our foray into the world of costumed adventurers and wrote a sly "Perhaps Vanguard could be a monthly article"; an encouragement from her to keep suiting up and fighting against bullies?

Fun Fact: Venus is the hottest planet in the solar system with a surface temperature of over 450 degrees Celsius (that is nearly 850 degrees Fahrenheit)!

CHAPTER TWENTY-NINE

The rest of the class went well, I actually worked on revising my prank article. Third period with Dr. Raines' English class was kind of dull. We spent the whole period in silent reading and then lunch.

Lunch was uneventful, but I saw the "bully club" eating together and without the pink girdle since we'd been interrupted before Ava could give it to them. I said nothing, but saw that Ava was simmering, but she realized this was not the time, she calmed down and we departed for fourth period when the bell rang.

Fun Fact: In *Sonic the Hedgehog* (1991), pressing up, down, left, right, A, then Start enters a Level select and sound test mode for the game.

iT'S FRiDAY, FRiDAY

Mike Ripley gave me a few dirty looks, but I was not afraid of him and part of me was hoping he'd give me a chance to test out my self-defense skills, but the opportunity never arose. Pre-Algebra was no more exciting than the silent reading in third period; math by any other name...well it is still math.

Fifth period came and Ava, Bryson, Evan, and I went to Dr. Raines for History. James was there and he kept flexing his arms at us to show he was not wearing the pink girdle. Now it was MY turn to simmer. Dr. Raines made it clear that Friday was a day for silence. We did silent reading (again), reading chapter one from our history books.

Fun Fact: The Solar System was formed around 4.6 billion years ago.

CHAPTER TWENTY-NINE

It was no surprise that a handful of students fell asleep. It WAS surprising that Dr. Raines did not seem to care; hey, I guess if we fail a test, it is on us, not him. James Lowes was one of those sleeping. Dr. Raines sat at his desk the whole time, reading a newspaper and generally ignoring the class, letting us enjoy the period our own way I suppose; reading or resting that is.

At the end of the fifty-five-minute class, the bell rang. James woke up and I gently tapped my friends and pointed subtly at him. He stood up and began to walk and then there was a loud

---

Fun Fact: The Sun is over 300,000 times larger than the Earth.

crash. James' desk had tipped forward onto the floor. The whole class laughed.

Now the reason why they laughed was because there was something tied to James' leg and also to his desk; a long, pink, girdle. James pointed at me and said "I know you did it!"

Now I am pretty good and giving the innocent look and Dr. Raines did not seem to believe it was me. However, as luck would have it, guess who just happened to be walking by at that moment? Yes, Principal Nottingham.

Fun Fact: The term Greenbacks for paper currency dates back to the Civil War.

CHAPTER THIRTY

FRIDAY NIGHT OUT

So this was how I ended up where I was on Friday; in the Principal's office, being stared at with his Medusa eyes and despite all outward attempts at appearing not only calm, but defiant, being afraid of a suspension or expulsion.

Nottingham had called my dad and he was on his way down. I had neither admitted nor denied I had tied the girdle to James' feet and the other end to the metal legs of his desk.

Fun Fact: Saturn is known for its rings, but Jupiter, Uranus, and Neptune also have them.

FRiDAY NiGHT OUT

Whether or not it was me, Ava, Evan, or Bryson will never be fully learned or revealed.

To answer Principal Nottingham's question of how I would talk my way out of this, I merely asked him "What makes you think it was me?" I had watched a lot of television crime shows, so I added quickly "You have no proof sir, no one can say I did it, there is reasonable doubt."

He said nothing, but that was because my dad was escorted in. He appeared angry enough that even the fiercest grizzly bear would probably run away from him. He looked at Nottingham and scowled and it frightened me even more than him. "I'm taking him home."

Fun Fact: Footprints on the moon will hypothetically remain there forever; there is no wind to blow them away.

CHAPTER THIRTY

Principal Nottingham said nothing as dad beckoned with his hands to follow him and I did. I furtively followed him to the car and got in, wondering what would happen next. I sat down next to him as he started the car. He then turned to me and his look was not angry, but concerned. "You okay Hugo?"

"Yes" it was all I could muster.

"I'm not going to ask you if you did it."

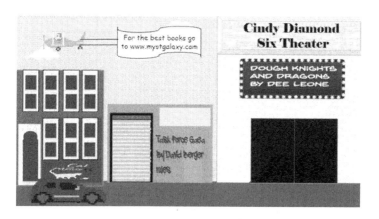

"Thanks." I was relieved at this and was glad not to be pressed for an answer. I tried never to lie to my parents and by not asking the

---

Shameless Book Plug: *Dough Knights and Dragons* by Dee Leone. Learn how knights and dragons CAN be friends!

FRiDAY NiGHT OUT

question, dad made sure I did not need to worry about it.

We got home and mom was napping (and so, I suppose was my little brother-to-be). I felt a bit overwhelmed, so I took a nap and then was awoken by a beeping noise on my computer. It was Ava.

"Hey, you okay?"

"Yeah, dad sprung me and nothing came of it."

"Cool, was it you who did it to James?"

"No comment"

Fun Fact: Around 70% of the Earth's surface is covered by oceans.

CHAPTER THIRTY

"LOL. Hey Hugo, by the way, I got tickets for a wrestling match, I really do not want to go, but did you want to take your dad? I heard he likes wrestling."

"Really? Is it the AWWF?" I asked, referring to All-World Wrestling Federation, the largest wrestling organization in the world.

"No, they are called the Professional World Wrestling Enterprises. It is some small one that has shows only in California."

"Oh, okay well, sure. I'm sure dad will take me."

Fun Fact: Humans have only explored about 5% of the world's oceans, there is a lot left out there to be discovered!

FRiDAY NiGHT OUT

We signed off after a few minutes. I went and asked dad and he became excited. "It is kind of like watching minor league baseball. You get to see some real up-and-coming talent...and a bunch of nobodies, but it will be fun."

We ate dinner and I changed clothes, this time wearing my Seattle Seahawks shirt, hat, and watch. That's right, GO HAWKS! Then picked up the tickets and went to the arena which as it turns out, was the gym at a local high school in the El Cajon area.

Once inside, dad bought drinks, foam fingers, hats, and all kinds of stuff to remember the event by and the two of us were totally hyped

Fun Fact: The F4 *Phantom II* was called "World's leading distributor of Mig Parts", because it shot down so many Mig fighters.

up for the matches. It would be a night to remember.

Fun Fact: The Pacific Ocean has more islands than any of the other oceans; about 25,000 of them.

CHAPTER THIRTY-ONE
OFF THE TOP ROPE

The first match began, a competition between "The Tigershark" and "The Beerbarian". It was a contest of skill (Tigershark) versus raw power (Beerbarian). The Beerbarian got the crowd rather energized as he began chanting "Brew S. A!, Brew S. A!" and the crowd began joining in. The match itself was also impressive, ending after fifteen minutes (The Beerbarian won by pinfall).

Fun Fact: It is rather common in wrestling shows for one patriotic wrestler to start a chant of "U.S.A!" The "Brew S. A!" is a parody of this.

OFF THE TOP ROPE

The time just flew by. Some of these wrestlers looked more like the "athletes" I would see at a bowling alley, with bellies hanging out a good foot or more past their belts. However, it was easy to forget this as each wrestler really put their heart into giving us a show that was minus some of the ridiculous, over-the-top nonsense you see on television from the larger name promotions.

It had come to an end and we were about ready to head for the exit, then the CEO of the company came down to ringside.

"Hello ladies and gentlemen, my name is Vance Cannon! I want to show my thanks for your

---

Author Fact: Despite not being a fan of "Heel" or rule-breaking wrestlers, my favorite wrestler of all time was Rick Rude. His "bad guy" spiel made me laugh.

coming out tonight by offering you one last match!"

The arena went dark and then there was a series of strobe lights flashing everywhere. The lights came back on and the ring announcer had returned.

"Ladies and gentlemen, for tonight's encore match, we have a musical act to precede the entrance of the competitors. Allow me to introduce solo performers Ken Tucker and Sarah Loredo!"

Fun Fact: Ken Tucker and Sarah Loredo are real performers and friends of mine. Look up their song *Mr. Moon* on YouTube, you won't regret it.

OFF THE TOP ROPE

As they played, a tall, thin, but heavily muscled blonde woman strutted down to ringside. She ignored the fans' shouts and attempts to give her high-fives. She was quite clearly the "heel" or "bad guy (girl)" wrestler. Her name was listed on the board as "Mistress Demise".

"Her opponent, at one hundred-and-fifty pounds...Lady Pain!"

I did a double-take; naw, it could not be Lady Pain, my Journalism teacher. Then the curtain parted and I watched as Lady Pain came out...I could not believe it; it was her! My teacher, Lady Pain was a professional wrestler!

Giving Thanks: My friend Suelean allowed me to cast her as Lady Pain.

CHAPTER THIRTY-ONE

I whispered to my dad who thought I was kidding. However, as she neared the ring, she caught sight of me and winced uncomfortably. I assumed this was probably because a teacher moonlighting as a wrestler would not be acceptable. I gave her a small wink, then made the "zipping my lip" motion to let her know I would not say anything. She smiled at me and she seemed much more relaxed.

Lady Pain was not exactly an intimidating woman. She barely cleared five feet, four inches. However, she began tossing Mistress Demise around like she was a feather.

Fun Fact: In *Sonic the Hedgehog* as well as the game *Starflight* (1991) for the Sega Genesis, if you did not move your character, your character would start tapping his feet impatiently.

OFF THE TOP ROPE

It seemed very one-sided and I cheered louder than probably anyone in the building, happily anticipating my teacher gaining a victory I would remember (but never talk about) forever.

However, Mistress Demise was not alone. Another person, a tall, thin man came down to ringside wearing a suit and sporting a haircut that looked like it had escaped from the 1980s. The crowd booed him and it became clear that he was some kind of ally to Mistress Demise. My dad was a huge wrestling fan as I said, but I knew very little about it. That said, it looked like whoever this man was, he had come down too late to help Mistress Demise.

Fun Fact: The famed 1934 picture of the Loch Ness Monster was reported as a fake in the *Sunday Telegraph* newspaper in 1975.

CHAPTER THIRTY-ONE

Lady Pain climbed to the top turnbuckle and I heard the crowd yell "Pain Splash! Pain Splash! Pain Splash!" She raised her arms above her head and bent her knees, flexing to leap off the turnbuckle and land on mistress Demise; finishing her off.

Then the mysterious, hated man in the tuxedo snuck up behind her and whacked her from behind with his briefcase. She came plunging downwards and collided with the referee whom was knocked out cold. Lady Pain looked hurt; lying on the mat, not moving and apparently quite stunned.

Fun Fact: Real or not, reports of the creature known as *Bigfoot* have been recounted for hundreds of years.

OFF THE TOP ROPE

The man walked over to the timekeeper and snatched the bell away from him. He then climbed to the top turnbuckle. I could not believe it; he was going to jump off of the turnbuckle and smash the bell into Lady Pain! What was he thinking? He was not only cheating, but he could hurt her really bad.

"NO!" I shouted. I do not know what possessed me, but before anyone (my dad included) could stop me, I vaulted over the small barrier in front of my row, and to the steps outside the ring.

Fun Fact: The discovery of the antibiotic Penicillin was in 1928. Its discovery by Scottish scientist Alexander Fleming was considered to be an accident.

CHAPTER THIRTY-ONE

I admit I had abandoned any resemblance to common sense. I was standing underneath this man and looked up at him as he prepared to vault off the top rope and smash the bell into my teacher and without thinking, I angrily shoved him from behind, the same way that he had shoved Lady Pain.

He came crashing down and his head struck the bell on the way down and landed on Mistress Demise. The noise his head made when it struck the bell awoke the referee who did not see me

Fun Fact: The timekeeper's bell has been quite a weapon in the history of professional wrestling, used as a foreign object by the bad guy (Heel) wrestlers.

OFF THE TOP ROPE

as I had been snagged by a pair of security guards. He only saw the man in the tuxedo lying on top of Mistress Demise. He rolled him off of her and shoved his prone body out of the ring.

The referee turned to see Lady Pain standing triumphantly on top of Mistress Demise and he counted "1...2...3!" The match was over! Lady Pain had won the final match of the night. She looked over the crowd, her face one filled with puzzlement. Her confused look grew larger when she saw me being led away (my father in tow) by security.

Fun Fact: The 1988 video game *The Main Event* used wrestlers that bore very close resemblance to real-life wrestlers. It is one of my favorite video games.

EPILOGUE

EPILOGUE

My father and me were actually jubilant on the drive home. We could not wait to tell our mom and my little brother. I had been taken away by security, but then Lady Pain had come into the security room, accompanied by Vance Cannon, Mistress Demise, and the man in the black tuxedo, whom I learned was named Gary Schuyler; actually a retired former preliminary wrestler.

I was frightened of Mr. Schuyler, who had a small ice pack held to his forehead, but he was laughing. Lady Pain had explained that I was one

---

Fun Fact: In real life, Gary Schuyler is a friend of mine who I cast as a character in this book for fun. Thanks Gary!

of her students at school and apparently did not have any clue that professional wrestling is choreographed to make it more entertaining. Mistress Demise and Mr. Schuyler were actually good friends and his attack of her was all part of the performance.

Yes, I really had been that naïve. I had been worried that Mr. Vance Cannon might decide to press charges or sue me for ruining his show. Instead, he was smiling brighter and wider than anyone. He then told me that I had

---

Fun Fact: The first "heel" wrestler is believed by many to be "Gorgeous George"; he began wrestling in the 1940s.

inadvertently given one of his matches probably the most interesting endings ever and that the publicity alone would sell thousands of tickets!

He shook my hand with a smile, while Mr. Schuyler patted me on the shoulder and said "Great match!" Lady pain introduced herself to my dad and they shook hands as well.

I looked at Lady Pain, a woman who did not want publicity I knew. I had wondered if they knew she was called Lady Pain at school, someone had to have known she was a wrestler, but she probably didn't want the whole school to know. She instead smiled and said "It's ok, I

Classic Game: *Law of the West* (1985) for the Apple II and Commodore 64 by *Accolade*. Check it out, it is fun!

don't see how it can hurt now." I knew of course that she would NOT want me to write an article about it; nor would I.

So, after all that, I left with a carload of souvenirs and a printed certificate that showed me as a member of Lady Pain's "stable", along with a one-year front row seat to future matches; with the proviso that I might be asked to step in again someday; that made me smile.

HUGO FINLEY:
BODYGUARD, ASSOCIATE
MANAGER FOR LADY
PAIN

PWWE

At the end of the night I got home and we shared our adventure. Mom looked incredulous and I could not tell if she was more proud or

---

Fun Fact: Wrestler "Andre the Giant" was often called "The Eighth Wonder of the World"; he was 7'4 and weighed over 500 lbs!

angry of my actions, but she merely said "Tell your little brother."

So, with the end of the night coming up, I told the entire tale to my brother and I had the surprise pleasure of feeling him kick against my cheek which was on mom's belly. We all laughed and smiled; what a great end to an amazing night.

I finally began yawning, so it was time for sleep. I took a shower and crawled into bed; which is where I am now. My dad always used to share his favorite quote with me, and it filled my head; "So we beat on, boats against the current, borne back ceaselessly into the past"

Fun Fact: The quote above is from the novel "The Great Gatsby" (1922) by F. Scott Fitzgerald.

YEP...ALMOST THE END

I am not sure where he got it from, but I was thinking instead of my future. I would have baseball practice tomorrow. Then Sunday I would play, and maybe I would get to pitch again, or I could play Center Field, or wherever Coach Bob put me. Then I would return to school. It had been a crazy week, but it had also been exciting, filled with strange adventures and new friends, and whatever happened, I would be ready.

The last thing I thought before I went to sleep was I'd have one doozy of a tale to tell my little brother someday.

Fun Fact: On my iPhone, I have Siri set to speak with an Australian accent just for fun.

AFTERWORD

As I bring this book to a close, I wanted to make one final remark. I earlier made several comments on bullying and without sounding preachy, I implore my young readers to keep in mind that bullying, even verbal bullying is not a harmless act. The results of bullying can stay with a child well into adulthood.

There is a good person in each of you, including people whom you may not like. Please try to see that person in everyone, the world will be an infinitely better place for it.

That said, I hope you enjoyed this first book in the *Middle School Madness* saga. I have another one in the planning stages with a return

---

Fun Fact: Bees change their brain chemistry based on their job. If they change tasks, their brain chemistry changes too! It is worth noting that bees can recognize human faces too.

AFTERWORD

of Hugo Finley as well as both old and new friends (and enemies).

FAREWELL FROM HUGO AND HIS FRIENDS — UNTIL THE INEVITABLE SEQUEL, THEY SAY "JOURNEY ON."

R. D. Trimble

Stay Tuned: Look for the next Hugo Finley book in 2019!

71930350R00177

Made in the USA
San Bernardino, CA
21 March 2018